Land Swap For Death

LAND SWAP FOR DEATH

Gregory C. Randall

For John D. MacDonald,
he was the best.

1a

Despite the incessant warnings to report abandoned or suspicious packages, things left lying about the BART platform don't last long. Commuters and tourists alike are ready to score a freebee: a lost iPod, a trashy book, Bra Busters hidden in the folds of the Economist, a cell phone with cool apps. All fair game.

"FREMONT . . . 6 CAR TRAIN, FREMONT . . . 6 CAR TRAIN," the red bead of overhead lights silently announced the next train.

"Damn it," she said. "Even tonight it happens, goddamnit."

She was neither tall nor thin but wide in the right places, well proportioned, and from a certain angle looked crafted, shaped, and taut. She knew she was still worth a second look.

She leaned into the wind of the on-coming train. The oily column of humid air, pushed by the oncoming train from the tunnel to the Montgomery Street Station, blew her damp brown hair, mostly hidden under a large hat, in tangled strings from her face; a few stray strands stuck to her sweaty forehead before the whooshing wind dried them. She brushed them away with her free hand. It was always hot on the Embarcadero Station platform when it rained, even in a San Francisco winter. The great hat hid her eyes.

"Damn it, goddamnit," she repeated. No one heard her over the mechanical growling of the train as it slid to a stop. She turned away and slumped onto the cold marble bench, and pulled her handbag tightly against her chest. With her right arm she crushed a brown paper bag tightly over the handbag. "Safeway" printed on the bag peeked over her arm in red three inch letters. The arm of her black leather rain slicker hid the rest of the words on the bag.

Her hair once again stuck to her forehead; hot flash, she knew that wasn't going to happen, just sweat. She might have been, at one time, cute, almost pretty; but that was an impossible story two decades ago. She fought the gray at her temples with dyes and brushed on color but in time, the gray would win. Her fight was with more than hair color.

She also hated the sensible shoes she had to wear—too sensible, too simple, too comfortable. But if needed in an emergency, she wanted speed.

No jewelry. Only a watch buckled to her right wrist—gold bezel, Roman numerals on a white face, a lizard band and gold clasp. The station's overhead lights were not kind to her tired face. Her exhaustion sat next to her brooding on the cold marble bench, taking quick furtive looks over its shoulder. Her fingers were long, and unlike most women, she wore no rings.

The train destined for Fremont left the platform, its two red lights rapidly disappearing into the dark tunnel that slipped under San Francisco Bay. She wondered if the train had turn signals. That brought a smile, her first all day.

The far end of the platform was empty and quiet as the chattering wheels died away. She usually sat mid-platform this time of night. Tonight she had perched on the round stone bench at the farthest end of the platform, near the winding stair she'd come down.

Her nose flared at the assault on her senses. "God, what stinks?" she swore under her breath. The dry and machine-oily air was overpowered by an outrageous stench—as if the offal and urine of a Tenderloin back alley had been shoveled in a bag and dumped over the dark shape fixed in place in front of her. A man, his face as dark and grimy as the blackness of the tunnel under the Bay, stood unsteadily in front of her. He was slightly hunched, layers of rags hanging from his shoulders; his shoes wrapped in duct tape. She thought he was a real zombie whose listless and unfocused eyes wandered from her breasts, to her face, and then back to her breasts. She pulled her arms more tightly around the bag unaware of pushing her bosom into greater prominence. She felt a small bead of sweat rolled down her neck, hold for a moment, then slide along her cleavage to settle near her lungs. She wanted to scream. Not tonight—no, she couldn't scream—not tonight.

She pushed slightly with two fingers against her chest to blot the dampness. He stared not at her breasts; it was the bag that held his lewd attention.

She shifted the bag to her right, under her slicker, trying to protect it. This freed her left arm—just in case she needed it. He watched the bag disappear.

"Damn it, get the hell out of here," she said, just loud enough to be heard over the background din.

He mumbled something incomprehensible.

"Jimmy say gi'me a fu'king pull from your bottle, lady," he repeated with enough vowels to connect the other letters.

She rose from the marble using her left hand for balance. Exhaustion remained on the bench, passed-out from fear, a puddle forming under its seat. She spun on her sensible heels, and headed toward the middle of the platform. Jimmy's eyes followed her, his voice chased her.

"Howz-about a pull from your fu'king bottle, lady? A goddamn drink, just a little one, Jimmy needs a tasty, bitch. Or ar' ya too goody-good for me?"

His words kicked her faster down the platform as she fled back into the herd. She moved into the shadow of a large white man—he turned away, ignoring her. Two short toots signaled the hope imminent escape.

"BAY POINT . . . 6 CAR TRAIN, BAY POINT . . . 6 CAR TRAIN," the lights flashed—salvation.

"Thank God," she whispered and quickly lined up behind the orange and black floor markings where a train door would soon arrive.

The tunnel wind again blew her hair away from her face. She turned to confirm the bum was gone—then gasped, finding him immediately behind her, one hand spastically rubbing his face. He stared at the bag, her eyes, the bag, her eyes.

"A pull from your fu'king bottle, girly goody-good," he spit between the stained fingers muffling his drooling mouth. "Com'on bitch, gi'me a drink." The man and the teenagers queued ahead of her quickly looked away, ignoring the drama, hoping the door would open in time to save them. The train stopped; the wind died. His stench pummeled her nose again and stung her eyes; nausea roiled her stomach.

The train car doors slid open with a sucking sound. The line of the intentionally uninvolved anxiously pushed their way into the already packed car. None turned to watch—they were now safe. This late in the evening the cars were always full before they reached the Embarcadero Station. The reasons given for not having enough seats: budget cuts, economization, poor ridership—bureaucracy was probably the prizewinner.

The woman stumbled onto the train and stood, cramped, among the last passengers at the door, facing out. Heat and steam filled the train car from the rain-soaked passengers. The sliding doors stood open. The bum, only a step away on the mustard yellow floor dots, stared at the bag.

The car's alert sounded with a "Bing." "The doors are closing. Please stand clear of the doors," a nasal voice intoned over the speakers.

She tried to relax, but to her horror the man's arm, snake-like, struck out from deep within the bundle of rags, ripping the bag from her arms just as the sliding doors met.

Her handbag fell toward the floor, but stuck between her hip and the closed door. Again a scream froze in her throat. She couldn't move; she could only glare at the bum's back as the train accelerated away from the platform and into the tunnel under the Bay. Her reflection on the door's windows stared back at her.

Goddammit, he stunk real, acted real, maybe he was real. Are they on-to-me, was I set up, busted? Damn it. She only had her mirrored face as a companion until West Oakland Station.

"Goddamn fu'king goody-good," commuters heard the bum mumble as they waited for the next train. "Where's my fu'king drink bitch, you take my bottle? Dat'z my bottle, bitch," he spit. "It's my bottle." He fumbled with his prize pushing his head deep into the open bag. "Where's the bottle? Goody-good take my fu'king bottle? Bitch."

He threw the bag onto the floor. It slid across the sticky ter- razzo and slammed into a marble bench. The bag split open, dumping bundles of papers into a chaotic mess.

"Piss on it, fu'k it and the mother-fu'king goody-good too." His eyes passed over the crowd. They turned as if avoiding eye contact were a way to remain invisible to the pile of rags limping back to the dark end of the platform.

1b

Richard Franklin worked late; he always worked late. His wife made an issue of his hours—but never his salary. She en- joyed their life, though he didn't. At home she questioned every- thing he did, correcting him when she decided he was wrong, complaining about all the ills in the world—as if each one were a personal attack. The club and her friends were the life he provid- ed. She used them fully. He worked hard and provided well— she did neither.

He coasted down the BART escalator wedged in between the damp crowd above and below. He stood a head higher than most of the commuters. His crisp suit was sharper and his tie more striking than most on the escalator. His shoulders slumped as he watched the Bay Point train leaving the station without him.

Damn it. Missed it again. Franklin was always punctual, had memorized the train schedule the day it changed, but couldn't predict the timing of the crosswalks on San Francisco's Market Street. *Another twenty minutes to wait. Damn.*

Clearing the escalator he sat his briefcase down near one of the benches and shook the rain from the sleeves of his trench coat. He was careful so the spray didn't fall on anyone standing near to him. He was a considerate and attentive man—normally.

A few people milled about the platform, cell phones stuck to one side of their faces. A faint odor, almost a stench, hung in the humid air left by some passenger now presumably boarded or exited. Franklin rubbed his nose to clear the smell and opened the paper under his arm.

The news—except for usual disasters, disease, death, murders, famines, and celebrity parties—was sparse. What a sorry world. Maybe Anne was rubbing off on him after all these years; nobody gives a damn any more—he shook the thought out of his head.

Two toots alerted the station of the next train. The sign for FREMONT flashed overhead and a flush of warm air passed over the crowd. His wait was half over. The pressure wave kicked up a few sheets of paper and blew them up against his foot where he snagged them with his well-polished Allen Edmonds right shoe. Franklin watched the unrehearsed drama on the platform. He was always amazed how people jostled and squeezed into the nearly packed cars—with backpacks, shopping bags, and wheeled luggage. He shook his head as four colorful spandexed swathed men pushed their racing bikes into the last car. The disapproval of the passengers was visible.

Franklin kicked the brown bag that lay against the bench. Loose papers spilled out adding to the collection pressed under his shoe—they were stapled, clipped or wrapped with rubber bands. He hated disorder to the point of personal discomfort. He railed about it at the office (where it was attended to) and at home (where it was ignored). He reached down and took hold of the edge of the bag. It resisted, then ripped, dumping the rest on the papers on the floor. He quickly gathered up the stack of pages, flattened them on his leather briefcase and peeled back the top sheet, exposing deeds, contracts, meeting notes, calendar logs and checks. All copies.

Copies had no real value—that he was sure of. They were neat and in sequence, and, from their smell, fresh. Their clean almost antiseptic smell of toner bled into the subway air. Why here? Dropped, dumped, forgotten? His forty years of accounting experience told him these papers represented a chronology of events and actions to *someone*. What they meant was a different matter. The name "Clayburn Company" headed most pages. The dates on the calendars and logs spanned the last eighteen months. The names on the checks included newsworthy politicians from the South Bay as well as various re-election committees.

Clayburn was a well-known Bay Area developer. Franklin had read about his business dealings in the *Chronicle* and other business papers. You couldn't miss his development signs all over Santa Clara and San Mateo counties. There were even a few near the train station in Lafayette. Properties for sale, new buildings for lease, and apartments for rent; he felt a like a voyeur peeping through the pages of another business's life.

A toot and a soft breeze signaled another westbound arrival from under the Bay. Franklin ignored the announcement; the train was from Oakland. "Nine car train for Daly City arriving on platform two." The cars jerked to a stop. He watched people exit in dark raincoats and ponchos. One person caught his eye, a woman wearing a slick black leather trench coat and a large hat. He turned back to the papers. A few of the papers now spread on his briefcase attracted his curiosity. He neatly folded them and slid them into his breast coat pocket to read on the trip home. He placed the others in the briefcase next to the insurance papers he had retrieved earlier in the day from his safety deposit box. Two short toots and "BAY POINT" flashed overhead signaling his train.

What the hell. At least I'll have something to read.

Richard Franklin, with an audible sigh, closed the briefcase.

1c

Franklin had a tough time keeping his eyes open after the long day. Fighting the train's narcotic affect proved hard. The pages of grant deeds, option contracts, and canceled checks between politicians and companies and Clayburn Development weren't enough to keep him awake. Most dealt with land in south Santa Clara County just off Highway 101. He recalled the undeveloped property, visible from the historic El Camino Real, from trips to Carmel and Monterey. This three hundred year old road, built in the days when Spain ruled California, ran from San Francisco to Los Angeles. It was the era when the Spanish were California's first developers.

The train passed under San Francisco Bay and then through Oakland before it exploded out of the tunnel cut through the East Bay hills and clattered downhill into the quaint village of Orinda. Franklin looked out the train's window and watched the cars on the paralleling freeway kick-up spray from the rain that sparkled in the endless stream of automobile headlights. He'd left the house that morning and, heeding the weather report, slipped on his dark green trench coat and stuffed the collapsible umbrella into his briefcase. This rain was welcome even though inconvenient—it would help to end the drought.

He shot his sleeve. His gold Rolex read 11:19. Looking out the window he noticed the reflection of a black leather clad woman walking up the aisle. When she reached him her hip bumped his arm. Perfume filled his nose. He paid little attention. Anne would be pissed. She seldom saw him for more than four hours at a time due to either her schedule or his. It reduced their time together to periods between events. Time together, just the two of them, never happened anymore. Later this month, after tax season, he promised himself to get away, just the two of them, maybe Paris or Hawaii. Anne still hadn't decided which or at least told him her decision. He remembered how he heard about the location of the last vacation—a friend's wife told him at a cocktail party.

An annoying beat began pounding the car's walls as two slackers, carrying a boom box, pushed their way through the sliding car doors. Franklin looked up; he hated rap music especially when broadcast by obnoxious teenagers. By the look of their tattooed arms, black baggy jeans, silver and black Raider's jackets, and ball caps turned just enough to give a cocky look, the skivers were nearly adults. They cased the passengers up one side of the car then down the other—then turned up the volume. They looked malevolently into every face that dared to look at them. Commuters try never to stare at the other passengers on a train; never. The hooligan's yellow eyes looked into every curious face. Like jackals circling a herd of antelopes, they looked for signs of weakness; probing with their eyes; using their music as bait. For a moment Franklin was pissed, but he let it slide: thugs, amateurs, hoodlums, druggies. They were nothing to what he had seen and dealt with in Vietnam. They were posers, scum, nothing more—nothing less. He ignored them.

He stuffed the papers back into his scuffed briefcase, closed the worn lid and pushed in the well-burnished latches. He had carried the case for almost twenty years; it was his oldest friend, older than his time with Anne. It held everything important in his life: account numbers, his diary, extra keys, blackberry, phone—it was his portable office. Anne said the case was disgusting. The new black leather briefcases in his closet, all covered in dust, attested to her determination to rid him of his most loyal associate.

The signs for Lafayette station flashed by on the platform as the train slowed to a stop, the doors slid open and rain blew over the first exiting passengers. Franklin opened his umbrella and stepped onto the platform; the cold wind did little to muffle the pulsing beat still knocking against his ears. He hoped the two thugs would stay on the train.

Most mornings Franklin arrived before 7:00 and had a short walk downhill from the adjacent parking lot to the station. His call to the East Coast office of his insurance company delayed him this morning. Tardy, he was forced to park in the furthest lot. Even with his umbrella, tonight's walk would be long and wet. He sat on a bench inside the station and slipped rubbers over his shoes. Franklin smiled to himself. Above him—brightly lit—a billboard advertised the town's newest luxury condominiums, proudly brought to Lafayette by The Clayburn Company. If he had made the 10:38, the sign would have made no impression; now the name Clayburn had a completely different meaning.

Reaching his car he was breathing heavily. The overhead parking lot lights flared off the two-month-old Christmas present to himself, a BMW 750i. It had been a good year for his business, his toys made his life more enjoyable. Pointing the key fob at the car, like a Star Trek laser, he gave a squeeze and the car chirped like a bird. It always gave him a kick. He squeezed the fob again — chirp.

The sound of flat soles slapping fast on wet pavement slowed his hand as he pulled the handle of the rear car door. He only had enough time to pitch his briefcase into the back seat before the two kids from the train slammed him against the side of his car.

"What the hell," he yelled into the face that pinned his forearm against his chest. "What the hell do you want?"

"The keys man, give me the fucking keys. Now!" the taller of the two screamed in his face.

"No way." He tried to push back.

"Listen motherfucker, give me the keys now or I'll blow your goddamn motherfucking head off."

Only then, in the glare of the overhead lights, Franklin saw and felt the chrome cannon held hard against his cheek. Jerking one arm free he grabbed the barrel and pushed it down toward the wet asphalt.

The roar momentarily deafened them. Franklin felt the bullet's searing trip through his chest, ribs, and abdomen. Then, looking for new options, it punctured the left rear tire of the BMW. He was already dead as the air simultaneously exploded out of his lungs and the tire.

The shorter kid, at the sound of the gunshot, ran to the passenger side of the car and threw the ghetto blaster into the back seat. The shooter pulled the keys from Franklin's grip, kicked away the body, jumped into the driver's seat. With practiced skill, he pushed the start button and felt the motor roar into life. With his right hand he put the car in gear and floored the accelerator. On damp paving a BMW with four good wheels is a handful; on wet paving—with only three good tires—it's uncontrollable.

The huge automobile lunged ahead and instantly began to fishtail. The killer panicked, over-corrected, and forced the car into a sideways slide; sparks flew from the chrome and steel of the left rear rim. The vehicle slid chaotically across the lot until it slammed head-on into a parked dark blue pickup truck. The BMW's interior brilliantly exploded and filled with the white, almost fluorescent, glow of air bags. In seconds the bags were gone and only two forms were left, slumped forward onto the dash.. Seconds passed and then, just as the driver began to recover, his door window exploded, throwing glass over the punk. He jerked upright and violently twisted into the lap of the second still unconscious thug.

The blinding rain increased to biblical ferocity, obscuring the crashed cars and most especially the sprawled body of Richard Franklin. His blood comingled with the downpour and flowed across the parking lot to a storm inlet that said: *"No Dumping, Drains to the Bay"*.

1d

Kevin Bryan hated rainy nights, especially those that involved a dead body. Tonight, a bonus: two dead bodies and a seriously banged up third.

After a twelve-hour shift in the Lafayette detective's squad room, and, hoping for a quiet night, all Bryan wanted was an hour with the latest Connelly book, warm Fig Newton cookie and a short whiskey. The combination always helped him sleep. Now, standing in the rain, no hat, no umbrella, cold water running down his back, and his brown leather shoes submerged under an inch of water, his is only thought was unrequited vengeance against those that put him here.

"Hi Jerry, what do you have?" he said to the officer standing over the body in the center of the lot.

"Dead white male, about sixty, well dressed, haven't check for an I.D., waiting for Miller. Dispatch said the deputy coroner was at a dinner party for some rich dude; politics or something like that."

Bryan wondered why anybody whose job was to cut up dead people would be invited anywhere, especially to a dinner party where everyone would wonder where those hands had been that day.

"What about the others?" he asked as they walked over to the BMW.

"One dead, looks like the driver, the other kid banged up, but no significant injuries. Seems strange the driver died, couldn't have been going too fast, there's blood everywhere," Jerry added.

The rain abruptly stopped leaving everything wet and shiny. Red and blue lights from the squad cars flashed off every surface. Abrasive radio chatter filled the silence with staccato bursts from the police interceptors of the Lafayette and BART police that covered the parking lot. Two Contra Costa sheriff patrol cars turned into the lot, their lights added to the party like it was the start of a parade, their white squad cars lessened the impact of the dominant black cars of the BART police.

At the ambulance the injured man moaned and rolled his head side to side. Bryan could see, as the lights played across the man's wet face, he was really a boy, white, clean, very short dark hair, tattoos on his neck and a dark bruise already forming on one side of his face.

"Condition," he asked, the attendant.

"Not too bad, face lacerated, probably from the airbag. No obvious broken bones but his internals need to be checked. Took a good wallop inside the car—no seat belt. Vitals don't seem to show significant trauma just shock. He'll be at John Muir Hospital in ten. They can let you know more after an hour or so."

"Jerry, what do you think?" he asked, as they walked back to the center of the lot.

"Bad carjacking I would guess. Pretty damn sure the BMW

wasn't the driver's. This fellow, on the ground here, was about to get in his car and was pounced by these two. He was then shot either in a struggle or just because these two assholes wanted to shoot him. We got a flat tire on the BMW, maybe it was also hit. The two took off in the car, lost control, slid into the truck. Airbags blew." Jerry's summery was good and to the point, the way Bryan liked it. The detailed report would come from the county's criminal investigators that would be arriving directly behind the sheriff.

"BART police were first on the scene, Detective Bryan," Jerry said. "Someone pushed the panic button up there." He pointed to the top of the lot where a tall pipe and box arrangement stood; its blue light sat like a flashing hat stuck on a stick.

"We also responded and were a few minutes behind them. After we walked the scene we called you. County was in Concord dealing with some flooding, they're only just getting here."

"Pass it on to them when the CSI's arrive," Bryan said.

The carved lines and loops in the pavement from the BMW's rim were still evident even on the damp asphalt. The BMW and pickup were connected with a looping string that tied the two dead men together. Bryan studied the body on the pavement and gently padded its lower back and seat; he felt the outline of a wallet. He slowly drew it out. He turned the leather toward Bobby's flashlight. Blood poured out, the soaked bills showed a macabre mixture of red and green. Bryan asked for a plastic bag and one appeared from behind.

"Good evening deputy coroner," Bryan said without turning around. He dropped the wallet into the bag.

"Good fucking evening to you too, Detective Bryan," answered Dr. Ralph Miller, deputy coroner and perpetual political candidate. "Don't you hate it when the wallet's full of blood, makes a civilized identification so much more difficult. It would be easier if they just left it out. Bryan, did you move the body to get the damn thing? Was he photographed before you pulled it? Where the hell are the techs? And Bryan, you know damn well that you don't touch a dead man."

"Felt for it and pulled it, too dark to see the blood with all this rain, forgot gloves," Bryan said. These days a cop never touches anything or anybody, especially a bloody body, without latex.

"Go to my wagon and wash well with alcohol and chlorine and some disinfectant I got there," ordered Miller. "I'll go look at the other one, you didn't touch him did you?" Miller stood over Franklin's body for a moment and then walked toward the BMW.

Bryan rummaged through boxes in the coroner's station wagon until he found the disinfectant. There was no sting when he poured it over his hands; hoping it meant there were no cuts or nicks. He finished and waved his hands in the air. They quickly dried even in the damp air; they felt cold.

Stupid stunt, damn stupid stunt.

He walked back to the BMW and watched the deputy coroner stand and back away from the door. Glass sparkled, like glitter, over the body. The kid's head was thrown back, his arm hung down his side. The fingers, slightly curled, pointed to the ground; bloody water dripped on the pavement from the tip of the index finger. Blood covered the lap of the boy and the floor of the car.

"He was shot through the neck," Miller said to Bryan. "Through and through, and it looks like the bullet ended up in the seat of the passenger. Blew out his left jugular and everything behind it, almost severed his head. Died fast, maybe instantly. Bled out quickly too, blood everywhere on this side of the car. Looks like the shot went through the closed window. Helps to explain the glass." Miller turned to Bryan. "One big bloody mess. The joker on the passenger side, was he hit?"

"No. No holes," answered Bryan.

"Lucky son of a bitch, looks like a large caliber gun, we'll find out. The slug could have easily passed through this kid and through the other. Maybe even through the door panel. We will look for the slug later." Miller continued to look into the front seat of the BMW. "Gun!"

Miller stood back as two newly arrived CSI techs began to take pictures of the interior. When they completed he reached in and suspended, on a pencil, a huge chrome cannon.

"Couldn't see it, covered in blood and gore," Miller said.

One tech spoke into a small recorder. The other took a photo of the deputy coroner holding the gun up like it was a trout he had just caught. Bryan prided himself on his memory and attention to detail, but reminded himself to get a transcript of the recording as soon as possible. He didn't want a copy of the photo.

"You think the old guy shot him?" Bryan asked Miller.

"I don't think so, no significant glass on the ground outside of the car. There are just a few shards on the ground. Anybody open the door before I got here?"

The BART cop, who was first at the scene, admitted he opened the door, just to see if the man was hurt. He saw the wreckage and offered that some glass may have fallen on the ground.

"How many times do we have to go through this?" Miller said. "Touch nothing until I get here. Got it?"

"Yes, sir, I just thought he might be alive," the patrolman answered. Bryan heard him mutter something about the parentage of Miller under his breath as he walked back to the clique of cops standing off to one side.

"The older fellow up there looks like he died very soon after he was shot. His body angle doesn't make it look like a struggle after the shooting. Let's take a look," Miller led the small party of techs and cops back to the body of Franklin.

The flashes from digital cameras helped to spot their destination. Miller changed latex gloves. He kept the old ones and put them in another of his never-ending supply of plastic bags. He knelt and firmly rolled the body onto its back. Franklin's eyes were open; his face frozen in fear and shock. To Bryan his eyes looked like they still held his last look at life. The rain started again and Franklin's eye sockets began to fill.

2a

Sharon O'Mara lounged comfortably in the back booth of Smitty's Restaurant. For the last hour she had nursed a reasonable cup of coffee and waited for Kevin Bryan. The waitress had filled it three times. Bags of heirloom tomatoes, white peaches, basil still with its roots, and the usual kitchen staples and a few tasty luxuries shared the bench seat. With the exception of the roasted chickens—all were out of season. The head office in Connecticut assigned her the death of Richard Franklin. Her job, during the past week, was to fit together the bits and pieces of the incident before approving or disapproving the death benefit check to the widow. Insurance investigator—what a crock! Her duties usually consisted of: reading the police reports, putting her spin to them, and then okaying the transfer of the funds. Seldom was a transfer denied. Franklin's death was obviously not a suicide—that's unless you believed being white, well-mannered and rich made you a target, and as such, committed suicide by success. *God, am I getting more cynical than my usual cynical self?*

Early that Saturday morning Sharon had said goodbye to Basil after putting out his food and water, strolled out of her small stucco cottage a few blocks from the Walnut Creek BART station and taken the train into San Francisco. The farmer's market opened early at the Ferry Building and was easier and bigger than the Danville market. Today was her every-other-week trip—a half-day taste of a vacation. She hunted through boxes of ripe vegetables and greens, found some excellent sun-dried tomatoes, and filled two small paper bags with morels and shiitakes at the mushroom stand. Two plump rotisserie chickens, one for tonight and one to freeze, finished her shopping. Re-usable plastic bags were stuffed with flowers and vegetables. They hung on the hook-covered tripod contraption of wheels and shafts she'd brought from home which made it easier to get her goods on and off the train. Now that the City of San Francisco outlawed plastic bags, she dragged along her own cloth and plastic bags.

Her appointment with Bryan was at 1:00. She munched on a cinnamon pecan roll and sipped Peets coffee—black no cream or sugar—and sat on the rough wood timber of the pier that led to the Marin Ferry. Sailboats, manned by early morning crews, were heading out onto the Bay. A few had hoisted their sails, even in the early still air. Too damn cold for her to go out on the Bay most anytime of the year in a sailboat. She never could understand the human desire to get as uncomfortable as possible—doused with frigid salty water all day while weighted down by a life preserver—then brag about it and even show off trophies. Stinkpots, launches, large motorboats—they were as close as she ever wanted to get. And even then there was that *mal de mer* thing you had to deal with. No, the bay was gorgeous to look at, even better to stay off of. For her it's the East Cape of Cabo San Lucas with its bathtub water, icy beer, fruity drinks, and huge soul-eating fish. *Yes, that's an entirely different watersport!*

O'Mara watched the small boy jump up and down next to his father, waving at the Crowley tugboat as it threw a three foot wake as it passed the end of the pier. The child bounced about—careless and free—then froze, staring through the rusted railing into the water below. He yelled something at his father; it was lost due to the bellow of the tug. He pointed through the railing. Then he grabbed his father's shirttail and pulled hard to get him to see where he was pointing.

"There, daddy, there. It's a shirt or something, all checkered." He continued to point. "There it is again. It's bobbing up and down. There, daddy, there, see, see. You see it?"

"What are you looking at Bill, where?" The man leaned over the railing, shielding his eyes from the sun rising over the hills above Berkeley across the bay. He squinted, then quickly pulled back from the rail and scooped up his son. "Come on, Billy we need to go! Now. Don't look. Now!"

"Daaaad! You said we'd watch the boats. Besides, I thought I saw a real seal."

"No seal, William. Time to go, now."

Billy looked over the rail again before his dad could turn him away. The checkered shirt blossomed in the swell and turned over. A ghoulish white face flashed in the sunlight, seemed to take a breath, then rolled back into the bay. It flipped again from the wake from the tug, but this time the face remained looking into the blue sky; its wide-open mouth full of seawater, eye sockets empty. A woman, trying to light a cigarette, turned toward where the boy pointed, and screamed. People dashed to the rail. Someone grabbed a life preserver hung on the rail. Sharon slowly put her coffee cup down, taking in the sudden shock of the body by the tourists. She sharply inhaled and instantly, as only the mind can do it, flashed on Iraq and the last body she saw floating in water. The Tigris, as it winds its way through the heart of Baghdad, is a dark gray muddy pesthole of a river. The floating Iraqi body had neither eyes nor mouth nor head.

O'Mara watched two cops push through the crowd—slowed by the twenty pounds of hardware strapped to their hips. Their running had the appearance of fully loaded mules.

"Floater," said the policewoman. "I'll call dispatch to send the fireboat. Second this month. What a great way to impress the crowds and tourists—one more colorful story to tell the folks at home. Went to San Francisco and all I got were the photos of a body floating in the Bay and a lousy tee shirt." She looked down the rail toward the hundreds of digital cameras and phones snapping shots of the body. "Looks like when the mayor walks by, all the cameras and paparazzi." Her partner returned with a length of rope, fastened a noose, and lowered it into the Bay.

"Got him. At least he won't drift under the pier. That should hold him until the fireboat shows up." He turned to the gawkers. "Nothing to see here people. Nothing to see." They secured the rope to the railing. Sharon watched the officers walk through the crowd asking people to move on and not let kids see what was in the water. All that did was attract more people to the railing.

O'Mara knew this was the surest way to not get them to leave. There's everything to see, everything to ogle at, a hundred tweets were on their way. At least the older folks kept the youngsters away. Iraq was different. Bodies pulled from the river were found because some kid landed on it diving off a bridge or a levee. Or it drifted to where the women washed clothes. Death sat on its haunches along the Iraqi roads, alleys and levees of the Tigris River, studying the refugees as they drifted by, looking for any hope it could wrench from their souls. The same river, half a world away, provided water for bathing, cooking and drinking to a shattered country.

O'Mara finished her coffee and watched the fireboat round the end of the pier. It slowed and a large man on the bow waved to the woman cop, who pointed to the rope and the checkered shirt. Two men carrying fifteen-foot boat hooks worked their way down the port side of the fireboat to join the first at the bow. The large man held a length of rope. A woman joined them. She fended the boat away from the creosote piers with another boat hook. After three tries, the men snagged the body and slowly pulled it toward the fireboat, but it rolled free. They hooked it again. The cops on the pier slowly played out their line until the tug's crew could secure the their lines to the upper portion of the torso and the feet. The crowd at the rail continued to swell. O'Mara shrugged her shoulders and almost smiled when she noticed a skinny kid with tattoos down his arms snaking his way through the gawkers. His fingers gently lifted things out of bags and purses, unhooking totes from carts. The kid turned toward O'Mara and saw her watching. She smiled, raised her cell phone and took his picture. He backed his way through the crowd and bolted toward Broadway. *At least his slimy work is over for a little while.*

The body was hoisted up onto the foredeck and a tarp thrown over the checkered shirt. In five minutes this operation would be all over Facebook and YouTube—nothing stays secret for very long in this world. As bad as the body looked, no wife or mother would be able to identify their man from the Internet shots—it was a man she was sure. But then again it was hard to confirm even this close.

O'Mara lit a Marlboro with a silver lighter, and tossed the pack into her bag. The white scar on her right arm, just above the palm, flashed in the sun as she pulled the deep red hair away from her face. The edge of the fog line drifted overhead, throwing thin billowing clouds over the Embarcadero Center. The morning sun shot its bright bands of light across the bay as the fireboat turned past the end of the pier and disappeared. With nothing to see the crowd quickly dispersed.

2b

Bryan walked into the coffee shop and headed straight to her booth.

"Good morning." He was his usual friendly self.

"Good morning, detective. You're late and I'm hungry and I need to get home to put these things in the fridge."

He leaned over and gave O'Mara a brief but professional kiss on the cheek. "I wasn't sure with such short notice you could get here this morning."

"No problem, I've only been waiting for you for forty-three minutes. Two more and I'd be out of here." She smiled and touched her cheek in a twisty motion and cranked a smile.

Detective Bryan called shortly after she'd talked to the widow. He'd invited her to tag along when he asked Mrs. Franklin a few more questions about her husband's death.

Sharon said, "Based on what I was told yesterday at the office and with what you've gathered, I also have to get together with Mrs. Franklin to go over some details. With you along I might get the answers quicker. We do it today or Monday?"

"Franklin was pretty spacey when I called," he warned Sharon. "Do we have to, I'm very tired," he mimicked Anne Franklin's vague response. "She sounded distracted. 'Sure, why the hell not—the sooner this is over the better.' She also has the mouth of a sailor when she needs to!"

O'Mara had received a copy from her boss of the claims filing from Franklin's attorney within twenty-four hours of the shooting. The first police report attached to the claim said carjacking attempt, probable struggle, shot point-blank through the left side of the chest and out the lower right side. The bullet passed through the car and tire, and was found buried in the asphalt. Franklin's death was almost instantaneous due to the trauma a large caliber bullet causes to a human body.

Reading the final police report two days later, O'Mara was surprised to learn one of the shooters died from a gunshot while siting in Franklin's car just after the carjacking. The second boy the police found in the car was badly injured, internal stuff—still in intensive care. First-degree murder charges were pending against the survivor. "One less thug," she had said out loud, "but the price paid was too damn high."

O'Mara and Bryan had known each other before her tours in Iraq as an army cop. Since her return and time with Professional Life as an investigator, they had worked a couple of small cases together. One was a high profile burglary, where a serious amount of jewelry and art was stolen from a home high in the hills above Lafayette and later recovered when a drug bust went upside down and one of the perps gave up the other and the stolen goods. O'Mara was surprised when the owners were more thrilled to get the stolen property back than the insurance money, often it was the other way around.

"I've a few issues and questions about her husband's recent increase in insurance coverage," Sharon said. "The increase hadn't been formally approved but was in the system—so we have to stand behind it. So why are you seeing her?"

"Loose ends here and there; my questions may not be as nice as yours. I was hoping she might help clear up a few of them. One confusing bit's about some papers he had stuffed in his suit coat pocket."

"You don't think she had anything to do with the carjacking?"

"No, she's a nice, but very transparent—rich lady that has trouble planning anything more than her next social event. I was thinking maybe she knew someone who knew someone who might have passed a word on about Franklin. Probably a wild idea on my part, but other things have led to other things, if you know what I mean?"

She shrugged her shoulders. "Yeah, maybe."

It had been five days since the shooting and Anne Franklin had been, by doctor's orders, unavailable for a detailed interview. Beyond the initial face-to-face contact and some short questions Bryan asked when he stopped by to inform her that her husband had been shot and killed, that had been it. She took the first interview better than he expected. But the policewoman who stayed with her said she collapsed in a crazed and very real state of fear and loss. Some sedatives she had in the medicine cabinet helped calm her down. He couldn't wait any longer for the follow-up and hoped it all could be dealt with at one time. With O'Mara along it might be easier.

"How's my buddy Basil?"

"For the hundredth time, he's not your dog, no matter how much you butter him up with biscuits and bones and baby-sit him." The waitress came to the table.

"Good morning Detective, what'll it be? Sharon's already ordered." Kevin lifted an eyebrow at O'Mara.

"Leaving in two minutes?"

"Basil? You know he dislikes all cops and you're on the top of his list," she answered with a grin.

Basil, a Rottweiler-shepherd mix, was a reminder of another poor police marriage—a quickie in the back of the training ground when their handlers were not watching the two professionals. Sharon just loved the pups and took the one that showed an instant liking to her. Basil became her most trusted partner and protector.

"Yeah, yeah—but he still loves me more than you."

"Only because of the gifts you bring him. A lot like your girl friends." She smiled sharply.

"Ouch! And totally unfair, even if true."

Over lunch they compared their schedules. Bryan called Franklin on his cell and asked about the possibility of coming over now. He crooked his head and held the phone away from his ear. "Okay Monday it is. 10:30 after you return from the doctor." He put his hand over the receiver and whispered, "Good God, maybe he's better off dead than having to deal with that woman every day. Monday morning okay with you?"

O'Mara shook her head yes and dragged a French fry through a glop of ketchup on Bryan's plate.

2c

O'Mara strode up the brick walk of the Colonial-style house, prominent in a tucked away neighborhood in a flatter area of Lafayette. She hated this part of her job, interviewing the next of kin and insurance assignees. It stunk. Four years' worth of stunk. There were always tears and references to the baser nature of insurance companies and the types of people who worked for such places—to which she agreed with more than she would ever tell a client.

Nice house: neat, orderly, well landscaped and cared for. Looking back to the street she noted this was one of those few times her old green Jaguar XJ sedan didn't look out of place. It belonged here, even if she didn't. As she admired her car, an inconspicuous gray Chevy sedan pulled up behind. Detective Bryan pushed the door open and pulled his way out of the car like an unfolding tripod, one leg out here, another out there, and finally the whole apparatus stood erect. He was too tall for the city-issued car. Getting in an out was both an adventure and a performance. Bryan waved.

"Good morning. Anything new or important?"

"We had lunch Saturday, remember? How could anything happen since then? Or did you have a date that made you forget you'd ever spoken to me? The office wanted me to do this interview, get it in the book, and then move on. It's still on the front page of the morning Times and selling papers. Big insurance payment is mentioned, all attempts to talk with Mrs. Franklin thwarted—their word not mine and who says thwarted any-way—and with all the lame cop shows on TV about murders and payments, my boss just wants it over. If one more press babe calls her trying to earn her pay, she is going to explode and prob-ably all over me."

Bryan stepped back and put his hands up, "Whoa there, I'm just a cop doing his job, awfully short this morning, aren't we. So please just be pleasant, okay?"

O'Mara's cheeks flushed, "Sorry, been a rough morning already. Cuts at the office, five more gone, furloughed, fired—whatever you call it. And Missy Jane, the boss, took on an atti-tude about this settlement. So I'm here wondering if there's any support for what I'm doing. And if a week from now, I'll even have a job."

"Work takes your mind off it. Some days that's all I can do."

"Sure. Shall we?"

Sharon turned to the broad white paneled door and pushed the doorbell. A soft chime responded. She was fortunate Mrs. Franklin was home when she'd called earlier.

"Good morning, Mrs. Franklin," she'd said. "I hope I'm not calling at an inappropriate time, but unfortunately I must talk to you regarding your settlement and the disbursement of the ben-efits from your late husband's policy." Her's was a civil follow up to Bryan's Saturday call.

"I understand," a soft, nasally voice responded. "Would 10:30 be convenient for you? A Detective Bryan also called. If he doesn't mind I can meet with both of you at that time. I'm leaving for the desert after the memorial service tomorrow and I'd like to complete what is necessary before I go."

"Thank you, Mrs. Franklin. I know Detective Bryan. That should not be a problem. Yes, 10:30 will be fine."

After she hung up, she thought about how Anne Franklin sounded. Well educated from the accent, eastern schools prob-ably, but California had softened the crispness and nasal tones caused by sealed overheated private schools where the gene pool seemed to get shallower every year.

Now, at 10:25, one week after he was killed, she stood on the deceased Mr. Richard Franklin's front porch to discuss the recent increase in his life insurance from five hundred thousand to one million dollars. A woman like Anne Franklin would probably burn through even that money in a couple of years.

O'Mara heard, from inside, sharp footsteps on stone getting louder. With a click the door opened. A short, very thin Latin woman stood before them.

"Senorita O'Mara and Senior Bryan, good morning," she said in a heavy but educated accent, "Senora Franklin is expecting you." She led them through the foyer and then down the hall toward a brightly lit room with butter yellow walls, crisp white trim and a high paneled ceiling that sat like a hat over the couch and chairs. A thick red oriental carpet tied the room together. No flat screen TV ruined the look. A tall, leggy woman stood, back lit, in the far end of the room near the fireplace. Her narrow back was to them. Smoke from a thin cigarette surrounded and twisted about her styled hair like fog whispering in and around the north tower of the Golden Gate Bridge. She turned to the pair.

"Mrs. Franklin, I'm Sharon O'Mara with Professional Life," she extended her hand. "I believe you've met Detective Kevin Bryan with the Lafayette Police Department. Thank you for seeing us." Bryan, surprised by O'Mara's professional sheen, turned back to Franklin. The smoke drifted out an open window.

Anne Franklin scowled. The cigarette glowed in her hand, her eyes were red, her gaze drifted. Sharon knew she wore an expensive suit—St. John, but could never afford one. And the jewelry—all of the jewelry—simple, elegant, refined; quite proper attire for a Lafayette socialite wife of a rich gunned-down husband.

"Yes, nice to see you again, Detective, I'm sure. It is more pleasant here certainly than in that place you call a police station. Please come in and sit." She waved the cigarette toward the couch and chairs in the center of the living room.

Leading the way with Bryan close on her heels, O'Mara turned her head toward Bryan with a questioning look. The colonial interior expensively complemented the colonial exterior, a collector's assembly of pieces. Even to O'Mara's untrained eye she could tell these pieces hadn't come from Ethan Allen. They were the real thing, especially the Windsor chairs.

Mrs. Franklin again waved her cigarette toward a pair of dark red upholstered wingback chairs. Her guests took their assigned seats. Franklin sat in the red chintz couch that almost spanned the room. She turned to the door and to the small Latin women who had quietly reappeared. "Tea, Maria."

Sharon hated tea and she knew Bryan's preference for Irish whiskey, even this early in the morning. She noted the ice filled cut crystal glass sitting next to Franklin. O'Mara was certain it didn't contain Perrier.

"Well, Detective, what can I do for you today?" Mrs. Franklin exhaled a cloud of smoke. From the tone, their previous meeting and telephone calls had obviously not pleased her.

"Mrs. Franklin, I'm sorry there has been a delay in the paperwork releasing the check for the insurance. I'm unfortunately responsible for holding it up. Sharon, Ms. O'Mara, needs it to release the payment. There are just too many unanswered questions in this case. Until we resolve them, it may be a while before we authorize the release of the money."

A standard line in cases like this—drag out the process and maybe something will pop or change—all very official. When there's doubt, blame bureaucracy, act business-like, try to avoid emotional issues.

The tea arrived and the maid placed the tray on the low table in front of Mrs. Franklin. Maria then leaned over Franklin's shoulder and whispered. "Thank you, Maria, I forgot." Maria then handed her a small pen like device.

"My husband was a meticulous man and very thorough," she said as she poured, "and so is my attorney. He apologizes for not being here. He asked me to record this conversation if you don't mind. It is on now."

Bryan, taken aback by this out-of-nowhere request—he had never been recorded by an interviewee. He had no option. He shook his head yes.

"Thank you, Detective, for approving this recording." She smiled at O'Mara, "Miss O'Mara?

"No problem, Mrs. Franklin, tape away."

"Back to business as they say. Our family attorney found most everything in order. In fact this year's tax information was complete and sitting on his desk, though it's not due for another month."

Mrs. Franklin turned toward the window. O'Mara sipped her tea, Earl Grey. It tasted like perfume. One polite taste was enough—it would take the rest of the day to wash it out.

"You're aware Detective Bryan and the police are somewhat baffled by the events of that night," O'Mara said regaining Mrs. Franklin's attention. "They are not entirely sure the two thugs involved acted alone."

"Yes, I'm aware of that, but it will not change what happened. My husband is dead and my life is a now a complete shambles. Ms. O'Mara, I've only this house, some property, and some investments he made. Investments I didn't know about until he died. Your company's check, and it's my money you know, would be very helpful."

"Yes, I'm sure it would be," O'Mara said. She didn't have to tell Mrs. Franklin her employer's figures and estimates put his estate at over three and a half million before the insurance check, and he owned this house and one in Palm Desert free and clear. Anne Franklin could count on years and years at the country club and the desert without lifting a finger, as if she knew how. She could count on ten thousand dollars a month in tax-free income from the municipal bonds alone. Yes, Mr. Franklin did provide for his dear wife. Too bad they killed the poor son-of-a bitch before he could enjoy it.

The investigators found the bullet that killed Franklin—a slug that pierced his left side, passed through his heart and right lung before embedding itself in the asphalt beneath the tire. It was barely recognizable—only a small portion of the grooving carved by the barrel was visible. Its weight led forensics to believe it came from a .357 caliber weapon. The only gun found at the scene—the one found inside the car—was a chrome .44 magnum. A big gun for a little guy, Kevin remarked. Franklin's fingerprints were on its barrel. The bullet that killed the driver was also from a .357. It had passed through the glass of the driver's side window, entered the left side of his neck, passed through and then buried in the passenger's seat just right of the other thug's ass. Near Franklin's body, they dug a slug out of the asphalt that could have come from a .357. It was possibly the bullet that killed Franklin and flattened the left rear Michelin. The police were still confused about the timing of the events, and especially the missing .357. The survivor still had not talked, yet. He'd been out of intensive care only two days.

"Mrs. Franklin, your husband talked to our home office the morning of his death to inquire about the paper work to double his life insurance policy. He was wondering what was taking so long for the final papers—and the San Francisco office wasn't being much help. Our people here made some inquiries later that day and the main office reported the paperwork was on its way. They e-mailed him a summary and faxed the information the next day. No question he's covered for the total amount, but he didn't know its final status before his death."

"The underwriter," O'Mara continued, "who had talked to your husband, said there may have been a minor error in the old policy. Mr. Franklin said that unfortunately he kept the policy in his safety deposit box and would check it later in the day. Mrs. Franklin, do you have a safety deposit box at your bank?"

Mrs. Franklin withdrew another cigarette from her case and lit it with a gold lighter. "Ms. O'Mara, I couldn't find the key or the box number." She drew in and exhaled. "The bank began checking after my attorney inquired about it. Richard kept copies of all of his most important documents in his briefcase, including his diary. Unfortunately no one could find it after the sons a bitches shot him." She looked out the window and took a sip from the crystal.

"Richard never wanted a replacement, in fact over the years I gave him a couple of very expensive new ones, but he never used them. He said the case was an old friend; it brought him luck. Some goddamn luck!" Franklin knocked back the rest of her drink.

She turned to O'Mara and Bryan; her eyes were wet. O'Mara couldn't tell whether the tears were real or she was upset over losing her meal ticket. *Damn, am I getting cynical or what.* The thought marked the second accusation that day.

"I wonder where that damn thing is. We looked in his office. The police didn't find it in the car. That's what's making it so difficult to find the key to the box. I'm sure he kept the key in that briefcase. The bank has to look for it and then my attorney will need a court order to open it. I wasn't a co-signer—I've my own box." She turned a little more back toward the light. "He never traveled anywhere without it. I wonder where it went."

"Was there anything unusual," Kevin asked, "about your husband's investments? You know, the types of stocks, land, bonds, other things he may have invested in."

"Richard invested in stocks and mutual funds and some land deals with friends, always as a limited partner. They took too much time if he became more fully involved. I didn't know what he invested in; we seldom talked about it. He took such good care of all those things. I really didn't try to understand them, you know. Why do you ask?" The maid returned to the room with another glass for her. She took a sip and another drag on her cigarette.

"We found some papers in your husband's coat pocket along with the old insurance policy Ms. O'Mara mentioned," Bryan said. "Those papers dealt with a property in southern Santa Clara County. One page was an outline that described a land investment program and the other was a copy of a grant deed for a piece of property that could have been part of that investment. There were some assessor's parcel maps as well. Were you aware of any of this?"

"No, Detective I wasn't. Richard always brought home information like that; he has drawers full in his office upstairs. Some of these land developers were his friends and others were his clients. He was very selective though—in both his friends and clients."

"You're certain," Bryan continued pressing the point, "you weren't aware of anything in the South Bay, south of San Jose."

"Yes, I'm certain, Detective Bryan. Richard's last land involvement was in Idaho. He land was too expensive in California these days. He was waiting to see when it would warrant a long term investment."

O'Mara looked hard at her. Anne Franklin's eyes were drier, her tiredness showed. Her drinking also showed. The days had taken their toll.

"Mrs. Franklin," O'Mara asked, "do you know anything about a Clayburn Company in San Francisco?"

"No, I don't. The name is familiar but I don't know anything about a company called Clayburn. Perhaps from advertising on TV. Why?"

"Their letterhead topped the first page of the prospectus outline we found in his pocket. Mrs. Franklin," he continued, "due to the circumstances of your husband's death and the loss of his briefcase, we're still wondering why your husband was shot. As we said before, there are too many unanswered questions."

"He died trying to stop a goddamn holdup," she said sharply. "He was always saying if those bastards tried anything on him, he'd show them. He was a Vietnam vet, you know." Her jaw was trembling and she tried to take another slug, the glass was empty again. She reached into her sleeve, withdrew a handkerchief, and turned away.

"What bastards are you talking about?" Bryan asked. "What do you know about someone else?"

"You know, thugs like those two kids, anyone like them."

"Did he think someone was after him?"

"No, just the whole breakdown in society he saw all around him, Detective."

Sharon watched her closely. She may be used to the good life but sat scared now, really scared. She stood at the door of a future far removed from the insulated past. There was an abyss in front of Anne Franklin; she tried to regain control.

"Is there anything more you need? If not, I'll have to ask you to leave. My attorney advised being forthright and open. I have, but I object to the innuendo you're directing at my husband. To use the common vernacular, it sucks."

"There's no innuendo, Mrs. Franklin." Bryan gripped the arms of the chair to rise. "We have two dead people, one more in the hospital, a shot up car, papers where they aren't supposed to be, two bullets, one gun in possession, another missing, a briefcase that magically disappeared, and a sudden increase in a life insurance policy. You're right. I would object to an innuendo in the face of all this bullshit, I would object to a whole box of innuendoes." His face blossomed, matching the color of Franklin's eyes.

O'Mara quickly stood up. "Thank you Mrs. Franklin for your time. You have been most helpful. I believe, Detective Bryan, we have another appointment. Thank you again, Mrs. Franklin." O'Mara took Kevin's arm and firmly pulled him the rest of the way from his chair. Kevin continued to stare at Anne Franklin.

O'Mara escorted Bryan toward the door. She handed Franklin her card. "If anything else occurs to you, please feel free to call me—at any time. My service can reach me day or night, especially if your husband's briefcase shows up. Again, I'm very sorry for your loss. Thank you for your time. I'll call you later to discuss the payment date of the settlement."

"Thank you, Ms. O'Mara," Anne Franklin stared at the detective saying nothing as he opened the door. He went first. O'Mara pulled the door closed behind her.

"Thanks for getting me out of there," Kevin said. "I was getting very upset though I admit I had no right to be. This case is all crap. No leads. No headway. After five days, a lot of frustration. Yeah, I believe her when she says she doesn't know anything about Clayburn. Franklin really kept her in the dark about most of his investments. As long as she could get what she wanted from him and life, she was happy—I guess. Her story hasn't changed much since our first interview the day after the shooting."

"How amazingly uncynical of you. When will you get a final report together so I can release her money?"

"At least another week. But it won't be final until we have the murderer or at least a solution to these two deaths."

"She'll be very pissed when she hears that."

"I'll smooth it out. No one at Clayburn has heard of Franklin. When we mentioned the letters in his pocket, they said Clayburn is involved with some properties in the South Bay, but were not aware of a new prospectus. In fact, one of their attorneys called the next day to ask if he could see it. He concluded the letterhead was real or a very good copy, but the information in the letter was faked, maybe intentionally fraudulent. His rationale was some competitor or environmental group faked the information to publicly discredit them. Bottom line—he hadn't a clue as to the source or who the author was." Kevin looked at her Jaguar. "Thought you'd gotten rid of it."

"Never. They don't make them like this anymore."

"You got that right, and there are plenty of good reasons why. I'll bet you spend more on tows than on gas."

"Not anymore. I'm in the aristocratic hands of Reginald now and he keeps it running. In fact I haven't stalled for over a week."

"Well don't press your luck."

O'Mara opened the door of the sedan, releasing the mid-winter heat that had built up.

"Hey, thanks for coming, really. I hope this turns out to be a simple puzzle and the few unmatched pieces we have will all fit. Click-click." Bryan wormed his length into the city car.

O'Mara stood next to the open door and watched him leave. She spun on her pumps, offered her rump to the Jaguar's leather bucket seat and took a deep breath. Yeah, too many pieces of the puzzle still lay about. And no one had even a hint of what the picture was supposed to look like. Even the corner pieces might be bogus.

She drove back to the branch and the office desk she used for her base of operations. She had been back and forth across the states—even to Europe once—during the past twelve months chasing down claims and filing reports. Being able to sleep in her own bed for as long as this case lasted was heaven.

Her desk, a delightful beige tank that may have been government surplus at some time during its life, matched the color of the walls and carpet of the office almost to a tee. Sadly most of the employees matched the furniture. She knew two by name and sight, the others knew who she was but seldom talked to her. She used her office only two or three times a month—they acted surprised every time she showed up. If she had known there was a weekly dollar pool that reflected her attendance, day and hour thing, she would have been surprised they even cared.

No telephone messages, three letters that were follow-ups to cases, nothing else. She often picked up her e-mail at home; her paychecks were automatically deposited. She still couldn't figure out why they wanted her to have a desk, but insurance companies had to have rules. She'd been with Professional Life for four years and it was beginning to get old. A friend from the army, doing well as an independent investigator, said Sharon's long legs and red hair were better credentials than what most guys could bring to the table. She would always be able to get into places that slammed the door on a balding overweight guy in a cheap suit. Her friend asked her a number of times to leave the insurance racket and join her, but, as usual, O'Mara was suffering from a severe case of inertia. Time to move on now, she conceded—somewhere out beyond the insurance roundabout.

3a

O'Mara opened one eye and waited for the world to come into focus. The other eye, hiding itself and hoping not to be called into action, remained buried in the sweet softness of the pillow. A black face with wet nose and brown eyes was staring at her, its breath like old chicken and a saliva trail hung from its lips.

"Sorry, I know you've to go out. Give me a minute, let's see if this body works this morning." Pushing herself up from the mattress she felt the parts begin to click and operate. Swinging her legs to the floor confirmed she could at least get vertical. Every muscle, even after six hours of sleep, felt stiff.

Basil backed away from the bed and ran down the hall and back three times before she could pull her robe over her pajamaless body. She glanced in the mirror as she passed the bathroom. "What a mess," was all Basil heard as he slid through the kitchen, dragging two rugs under his butt until he came full stop by smashing into the lower panel of the back door. She pulled it open and stood to one side. He flew out like a furry black ballistic missile. Landing in the far corner of the garden, he lifted his leg so fast Sharon thought he would flip over. Twenty seconds later he was at the door, rubbing his muzzle up against her thigh. "Bone?" The dog reacted like she'd whispered the poodle next door was in heat. He ran to the counter. Paws to the edge, he tried to levitate the bowl of bones. "Down. Now." Basil dropped his spastic butt to the floor, his black tail sweeping dried dog food out from under the stove, throwing it across the floor. He sat like the perfect angel he was, until O'Mara gently placed a biscuit in front of his nose and said, "Good boy." He softly took the bone and headed across the room to his stuffed bed. He curled his windshield wiper tail under his butt and cracked the bone in two. He never took his eyes off his mistress.

O'Mara set the coffee dripping and headed to the bathroom to shower. She wasn't a stylish dresser, but she still got looks from the boys at the pistol range. Physically fit and still trim, but dealing with middle age was just the pits. No matter what she did, her full figured Irish heritage came at her from both ends. Like most women her age she wondered about what to deal with next—hair, butt, breasts, weight, energy, sex life; that and much more and depending on the day and the order demanded. She pulled a crisp dark green silk blouse over her head then zipped up a newish pair of Calvin Klein's. Red shoes with low heels finished the visible look. Underneath was comfort and cotton—at one time she'd gone the thong route like girls at the gym, coming to the same conclusion most eventually come to—who the hell was she trying to impress? They were about as comfortable as holding a rope between your legs, and then there was that riding up the back of the hips thing. She once watched a few young kids clowning around in the plaza. One boy grabbed the red rope that had ridden up his girlfriend's butt to give her an idea of what a female wedgie was like. O'Mara smiled at the strange things fashion drives us to. Cotton was still the best.

Bryan made her copies of the papers found in Franklin's coat pocket. A strange mix of documents from properties in the South Bay area, all seemingly disconnected. She opened Google Earth on her laptop and typed in the first address. She sat mesmerized as the image raced across the screen and suddenly focused on the address. Land, open land, spread across the screen, she clicked on a dot hovering over a large building, "IBM" popped up.

"Lot of farm land here, fellow. Bet you'd like that." Basil was at her knee. "In today's economy any of this land could be in play."

The other addresses turned up within blocks of each other—some pretty large parcels. Maybe a few hundred acres in all.

Why the hell did Franklin have these in his pocket? The common thread seemed to be Clayburn. The name showed up on almost every document either by reference or title. But some of the dates posted on the documents were recent and some were from a few years back. "Connected disconnection. What the hell do you do with that?" Basil thought the question was for him, and cocked his head.

"Let's give it a shot. Straight to the horse's mouth as they say."

She typed "Clayburn Company San Francisco" in the search box and up popped the web site address and the office address. The web site assaulted her with Debussy—too many decibels pulsing lyrically through her amplified speakers. She forgot she'd watched a DVD on the computer a few days ago and hadn't turned down the volume. The music was the backdrop to an artsy-fartsy walk-through of projects for sale and under construction by Clayburn Company or one of its subsidiaries.

"They're all over Northern California, Baze: Sacramento, Bay Area, Tahoe, Monterey. Pretty pricey—but they look nice, very nice in fact." She noticed one located in Lafayette and clicked on its logo. "Not bad, but too many people too close together for us, right? We like our little bungalow for two, don't we?" She scratched the black head behind the ears. His eyes glazed over just a bit, and if he could smile he would have.

She punched the phone number into her cell.

"Clayburn Company. How can I direct your call?"

"Ross Clayburn's assistant, please." She knew from experience trying to get the top dog directly only led you down dead-ends and he's-not-ins.

"One moment,"

"Mr. Clayburn's office, Vanessa here."

She sounded like the first person who answered the phone. Is this some kind of gimmick to look bigger than you are? "Good morning, this is Sharon O'Mara. I'm an investigator with Professional Life. Is Mr. Clayburn available? This is not a sales call—it's regarding the death of a client."

"One moment please, I'll check." At least she wasn't given the he's-not-here runaround right from the start.

Click. "Ross here. How can I help you Ms. O'Mara?" Efficient too!

"Thank you for taking my call, Mr. Clayburn. I'm following up on a murder of one of our clients in order to resolve the settlement."

"Would it be the Franklin matter, Ms. O'Mara? I discussed this with a detective a few days ago. I tried to be helpful."

"That would have been Detective Bryan. Yes, it's that matter. Would you be available for a short conversation this afternoon? I'll be in town. I don't need much of your time. Say 1:30."

"Say 1:00. I have to be in San Jose at 6:00 for a political event, so the earlier the better to beat the rush. Your first name is Sharon?"

"Yes," she answered, disoriented by the ease of connection and his graciousness.

"Excellent. Lovely name. My grandmother's name was Sharon. Excellent. See you at 1:00 then, goodbye." The phone clicked off.

"Wonder of wonders, old boy, that's about as easy as it gets." She rolled back from her desk and headed to the kitchen for another cup of coffee. "Easy with the ladies with that grandmother line. Baze, this may actually be fun."

3b

O'Mara parked three levels down in the sub-sub-basement of the Clayburn Tower. The entry sign posted twelve dollars for the first twenty minutes: thirty-six dollars an hour or three hundred twenty-four dollars for a nine hour day. Then she noticed the smaller text below. Daily rate forty-eight dollars, monthly rates also available.

Well that's not too bad, I guess.

She hated driving into the city. Traffic is always bad, the streets perpetually in a state of ruin, and the cost to park—ridiculous. She usually took BART, but she wanted to check out Clayburn's Santa Clara properties after her meeting—and there was no public transit to the nether reaches of the county. Why she needed to see them was more out of curiosity than real investigative work. If the office knew what she was doing, they'd probably dock her pay or make her pay for the gas at least.

She had to change elevators at street level. A security guard sat at the counter and two roamed the lobby. She asked which of the elevators went to Ross Clayburn's office. He pointed to the last one, but asked her to wait a moment while he made a call. He requested her name, after the call he walked her to the elevator door, politely asked her wait a moment, and punched in a key code on a small panel. Clayburn's top floor office had its own express elevator. Of course everyone was vetted before they could use it.

Entering, she stood to one side expecting the guard to follow. He didn't. He wished her a very nice day, touched the one up button and watched the door close. She relaxed against the wood paneling and extracted a folded paper from her handbag.

The prospectus outline—a black and white copy from what looked like a color original—presented a full-blown development on the 2,350 acre property. It outlined the scope and general scale of the new development in a diagram that showed where the commercial space, retail stores, offices and at least three kinds of housing would be located. A complete and exciting new traditional community for the expanding city of San Jose, it read. Her very short conversation with a local real estate broker confirmed the area was prime for development, though no one had succeeded in getting anything approved. It seemed San Jose wanted development slowed or halted in this area of the county. It tried to interfere and hamper development agreements with any of the landowners or potential developers. He also said much of the area was still under county jurisdiction, and landowners were fighting battles over even small annexations into the city almost weekly. Why such detail for a development proposal if the city wasn't supporting the idea?

The elevator slowed. A soft voice announced the floor. With a chime the door opened onto a cool red and brown granite floor and warm mahogany paneled interior lobby softly lit by alabaster sconces on the sidewalls. The receptionist's polished desk of black stone anchored the center.

"May I help you?" the demure women behind the desk asked. Her striking oriental features added considerably to the exotic nature of the lobby. Her red high collar smock-like jacket and the tone of her "May I help you?" suggested she and the stone desk had a lot in common.

"Sharon O'Mara. I've an appointment with Mr. Clayburn."

"Thank you. Please make yourself comfortable." It was a statement, not an invitation. She touched a few buttons and spoke softly into her headset.

"Thank you."

O'Mara turned to the room. How to accomplish being comfortable with an overstuffed leather sofa—too low and almost impossible to sit in—two matching chairs, and a glass table more inviting than the upholstered pieces, she was not sure. Designers don't seem to understand how their spaces and furniture are used. Were his Clayburn's clients' dwarfs or children under eight?

"Mr. Clayburn will be with you in a moment." Red jacket remained curt.

O'Mara noted with amusement that, except for the elevator, the room had no doors or other means of escape. The walls, generously paneled with original California Impressionists paintings of the California countryside and mountains, enclosed the room with their faux visions of the state, The largest—easily four foot square—represented a Sierra mountain range with a small lake in the foreground. She squinted at the signature scrawled roughly in a corner in orange—Edgar Payne. She followed the art market—one of the few positive remnants of junior college—more out of curiosity than experience or financial ability, with weekly downloads concerning auctions and sales. Her gut told her this large piece of linen and oil paint could easily fetch a half million. She admired the bold and dramatic effect of its red under-painting. Old Edgar, now dead these sixty years, would be shocked to hear the price—could have lived most of his life off the sale of this one painting—but, like most exceptional dead painters, others lived off his bones.

A soft pneumatic air release caught her attention and, as she watched the opposite wall, a vertical seam widened. Sunlight slashed the granite floor. A well-dressed woman emerged and crossed the floor with a staccato gait.

"Ms. O'Mara, I'm Doris Morgan, assistant to Mr. Clayburn and Mr. Cimoni. Would you follow me please, Mr. Clayburn is waiting for you." She sharply turned with the mechanics and poise of a soldier and headed for the brilliantly lit opening. The strong back, well-toned legs, odd hips, and very black hair tucked in on itself, led the way. O'Mara quick-marched to catch up.

A hard and challenging woman, O'Mara thought, or incredibly repressed. She had an adolescent desire to stick her tongue out. She resisted with great difficulty, knowing at least three hidden cameras were filming their parade.

The door silently closed behind them. Ms. Morgan's pace, five steps ahead with the gap widening, required O'Mara to increase her stride and stay alert.

Morgan looked to be in her mid to late thirties and in exceptionally good shape. Everything moved the way it should—someone who knew her body well—but the headlight glare from the hallway ahead obstructed a detailed appraisal. More paintings lined the walls—some lit by sconces, others by gallery spots.

"Impressive collection." O'Mara had almost caught up with Morgan.

"Mr. Clayburn has one of the largest collections of twentieth century California art in the world. He's often invited to lecture on the subject." The phrasing was crisp as a tour guide at the Louvre.

They turned a corner and the view and the scenery changed. This hall was an extension of the first. Granite ceded abruptly to a deep russet and green carpet. Mahogany panels continued with hundreds of smartly framed portraits of buildings on both walls: apartments, condos, office buildings, R&D facilities. The titles on the pictures named the "Whose Who" of the semi-conductor and computer industry. A few were plans and drawings, but mostly they were photos of completed projects.

Centered at the intersection of two hallways rose a model of the building she was in, Clayburn Towers. The windows of the model glowed from an unseen interior light. If by now Ross Clayburn and his company had not impressed a visitor, they were impregnable. The entry and hallway had been designed to impress the bankers and local government planners who backed his business ventures and to piss off the competition—if they were invited this far.

Doris Morgan stopped in front of tall double doors and touched the plate on the left. They swung silently inward. She waved her hand toward the door opening. A contained smirk floated across Morgan's face as O'Mara walked past.

The view was spectacular, even by San Francisco standards. A two-story glass wall framed the City laid out in front of her— Nob Hill, Russian Hill, North Beach and on out into San Francisco Bay. There were no seams in the glass. It was as if she were standing outside.

"Mr. Clayburn will be right with you." Morgan turned smartly toward the door and left her alone. The tension in the air seemed to dissipate as if a breeze had swept it out the door.

"Good morning, Ms. O'Mara." The voice was behind and above. She turned and looked up. A very handsome, dapper man, mid-fifties, in shirtsleeves, cuffs rolled, hovered at the top of the stairs that led to the mezzanine. The tan framing his white mustache promised English sophistication.

"Impressive view, isn't it? Even I'm still amazed by it. Not many like it anywhere. Good afternoon, I'm Ross Clayburn." He started down the stairs. "Care for coffee, or perhaps tea?"

"Coffee, black please." Sharon met him at the foot of the stair and shook his extended hand as he landed.

"Great, I'll pour. Never found a tea that didn't etch my tongue, even after ten years in the orient." He motioned toward the leather couch that faced the view. "Please have a seat." He strode gracefully to the freestanding bar. The china, pure white, seemed to glow in the softness of the light from outside. He poured and carried the cups to the couches, placing hers on the low glass table beside her.

"What can I do for you, Ms. O'Mara? Your call suggested our involvement in this unfortunate matter with Mr. Franklin. I'm afraid I don't understand your desire to talk to me about it, but I'll be glad to answer your questions if I can." He looked directly into her eyes over the rim of his cup.

"Again, thank you for seeing me, Mr. Clayburn. I realize the police have already talked to you about the murder, but my questions pertain more to the papers found on the body. Blood stained deeds always catch my interest—especially if the bearer was a client. Do you have any idea why Mr. Franklin might have had those papers?"

"No, none at all. As we said to the police, we believe the papers are fake. The copy of the deed was certainly real, but anyone can get a copy of a deed through the county recorder's office. What concerns us is the outline. Most of the information is simply not true. Considering the current political and economic climate, we're years away from planning commission approvals on that property. These days, trying to get a development approved is a very long and expensive process. Three years minimum, more like five. That's a considerable amount of overhead for any company to carry, considering planning and design fees, engineering, environmental assessment and just the mortgage on the land. We must be very careful about the information that's released; otherwise we're continually defending incorrect or confusing information. The process is indeed very long and expensive."

"The rewards are eventually acceptable, however?"

"Oh yes, Ms. O'Mara, the rewards can be excellent, no doubt about it. Finding the balance between risk and reward is like surfing. Do you surf, Ms. O'Mara?"

"No, I enjoy the ocean more from the back of a boat with

a pole in my hand. Tangling with marlins is enough risk these days. I learned a bit about risk in Iraq." She waved the back of her hand for emphasis.

"So you know how the proverbial alligator can swallow you whole. More than one of my friends in this business never made it out of a recession. We have to have a gambler's heart. More coffee?"

"Yes, thank you. It's very good."

"Thanks. A good strong cup of coffee is my weakness. This particular brew is from my plantation on Kona." The telephone softly interrupted. "Yes. Yes, sure Allen, if you're available. Thank you."

"If you don't mind Ms. O'Mara, I've asked Allen Cimoni to join us. He is my general counsel and right arm, handles all the minutiae and much of the legal work. Sharp guy. Likes to see results."

The doors opened with a sigh and the impeccably dressed, impressively tall—six and a half feet at least—man with strong verticality and loose extremities took in the room with a glance. Allen Cimoni headed directly to Sharon O'Mara as she stood.

"Ms. O'Mara, Allen Cimoni. Allen, this is Sharon O'Mara with Professional Life. She's investigating the killing of that Mr. Franklin a few days ago."

"I'm pleased to meet you, Miss O'Mara. It's unfortunate the circumstances couldn't be more pleasant." His handshake was intentionally firm, a bit too long with a sliding release that held through the fingers. A contact too intimate for the circumstance he'd just pointed to.

"Yes. It is unfortunate, especially for Mr. Franklin."

"What can we help you with?"

Everyone's willingness to help at Clayburn put her on guard. "As I was telling Mr. Clayburn, I'm curious about the papers found on Mr. Franklin's body. They suggest an involvement with something his family wasn't aware of. Considering Mr. Franklin's business and investment history, it's not out of the realm of possibility he was involved in such a development as yours. We're pursuing that possibility. Under normal conditions, such as a natural death, it wouldn't be an issue, but a bullet through the heart does change our interest—significantly."

"As we told Detective Bryan," Cimoni's voice was resonant, but clipped, "we have no record of Mr. Franklin's name in our files or computers, nor on any land contacts. Not even among the other land owners and limited partners involved with this development. We've asked our partners in our other properties if they knew him. One person did, but only because they belonged to the same country club in Orinda. We find no involvement with this firm and if I may be so blunt, we're beginning to resent this intrusion into the affairs of the Clayburn Company, Miss O'Mara. We are also greatly concerned about where this investigation may be heading."

"Thank you very much, Allen. You've done a great job defending the honor of this firm," Ross said sharply. He turned to O'Mara.

"Ever since we were informed of the incident, we have increased our surveillance and overview of all our projects. We have not been able to find a leak, nor even a theft. Who created these papers is a mystery to us. Our security staff now feels it was a set-up. Mr. Franklin was an accountant, head of his own firm. Perhaps he was trying to create a financial fiction to tag along with the outline. Maybe he was working with someone else who had reason to create this fiction. It's a thought—mind you, just a thought." Ross walked toward the window.

"I do realize the basis for my questions is purely conjectural but, with two people dead and no evidence to the contrary, I'm checking for even the slightest hint of a motive. Insurance companies seldom pay a million dollars out of the kindness of their heart."

"Ms. O'Mara, I started this firm almost thirty years ago." Clayburn turned back to face her. "We would not be sitting thirty-eight stories above San Francisco without our thoroughness and attention to detail. We play by the book and it has always been rewarding. I follow everything this firm does, approve almost every dollar that goes out. We have no connection to these deaths and those papers. I personally assure you of that." The glare from the window behind Ross made her squint as she looked into his face. *This room is his theater and he`s a good director. And he's rehearsed well.*

"We do have interests in a large parcel of land in the southern Santa Clara County area. You already know this or you wouldn't be here. It's public record and general knowledge in planning circles. Our project is in the early phases of planning and design. It will take years before everyone with an interest is satisfied. Many don't want this type of development—people with political, environmental, even personal, axes to grind. We try to placate them all. You can imagine how consuming and expensive that is. I'm ready for more coffee, are you?"

"Thank you." Clayburn took the cup from her extended hand as he passed. "I was planning to take a look at the area this afternoon to get a feel for what all of this is about. Do I have your permission to see the property?"

"There's little to see, Miss O'Mara." Cimoni said wedging himself back into the conversation. "It's all agricultural fields, some steep rocky areas, and a few small, rundown farms and ranches. With all this rain I'd caution you against it. The ground is pretty soft."

"Thank you for the advice, Mr. Cimoni. I'll stick to the main roads. And it's Ms."

"If you would like a small schematic map of the property, I've one you could use," volunteered Clayburn.

"Ross, we have not made this information public yet. I would caution . . ." Clayburn waved him off. Cimoni glared at O'Mara.

"It's okay, Allen. I believe we can trust Ms. O'Mara's confidence." He looked at her unapologetically. "Am I right?"

"Yes, I'll guard it with my life."

"Oh, no reason to be so dramatic. Just keep the information to yourself. Besides, much of the information is quite general."

Clayburn pushed gently on section of the rich paneling. Other than horizontal and vertical lines fine as silk threads, the grain of the rosewood panel was unbroken for two stories, a drawer silently opened. He handed her a letter sized copy of a plan showing brightly colored areas, black lines and a table with land uses and acreage counts, most of the text too small to read without a magnifying glass. She took in the plan without saying a word, noticing the similarity of the totals for different uses to the totals in Franklin's outline. Fascinating. Someone's doing good work. More questions flashed in her head. She really didn't want it to be this complicated.

"Thank you, this will be very helpful. This is a very ambitious project, Mr. Clayburn."

"Yes it is. Our phasing plans suggest the last areas may only be developed long after I'm dead." He smiled. "Considering how long the approvals are taking, I'm hoping the earliest phases will start before I die."

The telephone, on the table next to his coffee, rang. "Yes Doris, yes, yes. Thank you. Tell them to wait; we'll be there shortly. And Doris, please tell security at the south county site Ms. O'Mara will be looking it over this afternoon. That's fine. Yes, yes, no. See you tomorrow morning." He turned to O'Mara, "I'm sorry, but my next meeting has started and Allen and I must attend. Are there any more questions?"

"No, Mr. Clayburn. Thank you so much for your time and for the map." She stood up and shook their hands, Mr. Cimoni's and then Mr. Clayburn's.

Cimoni stepped forward. "I'll walk you out, Ms. O'Mara."

The door opened as they neared the panels—expensive solution to a simple problem—if the power goes out, then what? Not something she'd choose sitting atop the San Andreas earthquake fault. They walked to the doorless elevator vestibule. Morgan passed them in the hallway. She acknowledged O'Mara, brief but cold.

"Ms. O'Mara, thank you," Cimoni said. "I hope to see you again under more pleasant circumstances." She stood in the elevator and watched the door close on Cimoni's face.

3c

Pulling out onto Battery Street her phone rang. She stuck the Bluetooth receiver into her ear.

"O'Mara here . . . Good morning, Kevin . . . Yeah, just leaving Clayburn's office, what a pair . . . Cimoni and Clayburn . . . No, I didn't learn much more than we already knew, but they gave me a map of their South Bay development . . . Clayburn's very smooth, very together . . . You're kidding, really! Where? . . . Along the freeway? . . . Yeah, I know where the shoulder widening project is . . . CalTrans worker found it? Amazing. Someone must have taken it from him, or maybe from his car . . . They didn't take anything? Checkbook, credit cards, diary, keys were all there? . . . Too strange. Hey, hold a second." She gunned the Jaguar onto the freeway. "Can't think, drive and talk at the same time—only two out three."

O'Mara listened as Bryan detailed how the briefcase had been found by a CalTrans highway worker along the freeway, not three miles from the Lafayette BART station under a row of oleanders that softened the edge of freeway concrete. It was impossible to see until the worker stumbled over it. He'd opened the unlocked case and recognized the name in the checkbooks from the news reports. He turned it over to the Lafayette Police Department early that morning.

Everything that, according to his wife, was supposed to be in it was. Nothing unusual—the fact of it made it unusual. Anne Franklin and her attorney had already come to the station for the keys to the safety deposit box. They were evidence, but she promised to return the keys later in the day—her attorney would be with her all the time. His diary added nothing to what they already knew. The day of his death he'd had no meetings and there wasn't anything in the case about Clayburn or any other land development. Interestingly, there were no fingerprints other than the construction worker's on the outside. Someone had wiped it clean.

O'Mara moved in and out of traffic heading south on Highway 101 toward San Jose. "Maybe what's not there is more important than what is there. Someone obviously took the case from the car. That someone opened the case and went through it. If they were thieves—or even partners with the dead hijacker—they'd have at least taken the checkbook and the credit cards. Not dumped it with everything still in it. So who took the case? Maybe there was something else in the case. Something that was wanted, wanted badly enough to leave two guys dead in the rain. Something worth killing for."

After passing the San Francisco Airport exit, she merged to the left, cut between a gravel truck and a Whole Foods delivery van, and headed south.

3d

The trip to southern Santa Clara County from San Francisco on a good workday can take an hour and a half. On a bad day you might as well stay overnight in San Jose and catch a Sharks game, enjoy a good night's sleep, get up early and beat the south bound traffic. Today was an in-betweener. Traffic slowed near the San Jose Airport, went to stop and go through San Jose, and died, dead-stop, at the city's south side. According to the immutable bible of CalTrans, Highway 101 must always be under construction somewhere. Today the orange vested princes of traffic declared Santa Clara County the winner.

As she drove south, the clouds over the Santa Cruz mountains thickened, darkening the western hills that kept the Santa Clara Valley from falling into the Pacific Ocean—a primal fear of Californians. The morning forecast had said rain in the late afternoon. All wrung from a warm and wet storm creeping up from the south. The local weather babe's map showed a band of clouds in the shape of a billowing spear thrown from Hawaii directly at the Bay Area. Sharon hoped it would hold off until she was on her way back to the East Bay.

She reached the exit on Clayburn's map two and a half hours after leaving San Francisco. She was hungry but decided to get something to eat after she had seen the property.

The exit led to an abrupt dead end and a fence. A contraption of orange slats, gates, and multiple locks blocked the road. The deeply rutted trail on the far side of the gate continued west into the property. The colored plan showed this as a future road, Clayburn's primary circulation spine that connected the residential and commercial areas. It would then curve to the south as it approached the hills. North along Highway 101 would be the industrial and office space. It would be a complete self-contained community. *How nice.*

She returned to the freeway and continued south to the next exit, a mile south, the southern limit of the new town. O'Mara again left the freeway. This exit didn't stop in a dead end but continued, narrowing the further west she traveled. She swerved to avoid pits in the road; some would have bottomed out her Jaguar.

She left the engine running, stepped out of the car, and immediately had to admit Cimoni had been right—her first step sank into muddy goop that oozed over her shoes, even here on high ground. Looking north the whole property played out before her, some areas with neat orchard rows, others open, fallow, maybe abandoned. *So this is what twenty three hundred acres looks like. It's a lot of land.* She held her phone up high to take photos, turned a few degrees and took more till she had a complete panorama of the property that could be spliced together on her computer.

"Perfect. Just perfect," she said. It started to rain, not hard—a light mist obscuring the hills to the south and threatening heavier stuff to come. She turned back to the car.

A whack and ding rang through the car's frame, almost immediately followed by a rifle crack. She instinctively dove onto the muddy road.

"Where the hell!" she yelled. A neat puncture wound gaped in the side of the car, about twelve inches from where she'd been standing. Large caliber, probably a rifle.

A second hole magically appeared about three inches above the first, followed by another report. O'Mara squirmed through the mud to the relative safety of the leeward side of the Jag. Two pimples with a hole in their centers protruded on this side in line with the two holes on the other.

"Shit, it is a goddamn rifle!" Still hugging the mud, she reached up to open the passenger door. She dragged her purse out and grabbed the Beretta. She threw the bag back into the car leaving the door open. The aloha rain was gaining momentum and she was getting very wet, very muddy, and very pissed.

O'Mara tossed the pistol onto the floor of the driver's side and started to pull herself into the front seat when another bullet slammed into the car. The rain, now drumming on the roof, almost drowned out the sound of another bullet ripping through the inside, rear to front, the windshield held. She slumped into the seat. The passenger's door was still open. She pulled the gear knob and gunned the engine. The wheels spun on the mud, the car surged and began to fishtail, the open door slammed hard and took. She couldn't see a hundred feet. She held on tight and regained control. A flash of lightening coincided with the explosion of the rear window. Glass sprayed over the back seat and onto her shoulders. In the rear view mirror she saw, behind her, the dark silhouette of a four-wheeler pulling out of a dense stand of eucalyptus. She floored the gas pedal. A stop sign grew visible through the rain. She prayed there wasn't cross traffic and accelerated through the intersection. The truck didn't even hesitate. It was gaining.

O'Mara reached for the phone but it was impossible to punch in the numbers with wet fingers while driving for your life. The mud prevented a good grip on the wheel. The phone slipped out of her hands and headed to the floor. Her red hair hung in tangled strands. Grit and water dripped from her nose.

The truck began to fill the blown out rear window. Between the rain and wind, the noise was deafening. Another stop sign was racing towards her. Go left. Now! Starting her turn well before the corner, she tried to slide into the intersection and spill speed. The slide was graceful until a pothole hung up a tire, twisting the steering wheel out of her hands. The car spun three-sixty degrees. The gun slid across the floor and slammed into her heel. The Jag was still heading in the direction she wanted—how, she wasn't sure. She pressed the accelerator but it wouldn't move. Her toe found the gun jammed under it. She was rolling to a stop. In one minute she'd be dead.

The truck barreled into the intersection and slammed on its brakes. O'Mara reached between her legs and grabbed for the Beretta. She felt it hard and wet, grasped it—and came up with her phone. Throwing it into the passenger seat, she reached down again and yanked the pistol free, clicked the safety off, and jammed it into the seam at the back of the passenger seat while slamming down on the pedal. The Jaguar stalled.

"Shit, of all the fucking times," she yelled. The 4x4 slowed to a stop a hundred feet away. O'Mara's view from the mirror was obscured by sheets of rain. The windshield of the off-road truck was black, the occupant invisible. It sat, a great predator, pointing directly at her. She could feel the eyes of the driver, and the truck seemed to be breathing in great heaves—until she realized that it was she sucking in gulps of air. She laid the pistol in her lap and kicked the ignition. The Jag roared to life.

The truck began to move—not towards her, but backing away. It turned around slowly in the middle of the road, accelerated, and disappeared into the haze of the rain.

O'Mara was frozen in her seat. Stunned. Her banging heart pumped adrenalin everywhere; she started to shake, her body becoming harder to control.

Iraq, the cold rain, an IED exploding two Humvees ahead, the dead child on the hood of her Humvee—the rain, the goddamn fucking rain—the blood running in small streams from under the devastated truck's carcass. The screaming she could see but not hear because of the concussion. The firefight, exploding windows, dead humans and ripped body parts everywhere.

The flashback shook her back to reality. She grasped the wheel, grabbed a deep breath, slammed the door, and put the car in gear. It eased away from the intersection. A quarter of a mile later, she wiped the rain and blood from her eyes, spit mud out the window, allowed another deep breath and realized she was still alive.

She maneuvered, almost willed, the Jag down the back road full of potholes and ponds, skimming across the storm water until a weathered and bullet-pocked sign for San Martin appeared out of the thick haze. A gas station materialized behind a dense stand of trees. O'Mara pulled in, and wiped her forehead. Shaking, she slid of out the bucket seat, stood, and, after looking up toward heaven so the rain could clean mud from her face, sloshed toward the office.

"You okay, Ma'am?" The young attendant looked shocked, he was unsure of what or whom he was looking at.

"Yeah, I think so, thanks. Small problem up the road," she said forcing a smile.

"Was there an accident? Should I call the sheriff?"

"No accident, but yes, please call the sheriff while I clean up. Where's the washroom?"

"Use that one—it's cleaner." He pointed to a door marked "Employees Only".

The image in the mirror told her why the kid was so concerned. She must have nicked her forehead when she rolled behind the car. A small cut had produced a lot of blood that had mixed with the mud and rain. It had run down her forehead, across her right cheek and settled along the collar of her blouse—creating a vision of mayhem and wreckage under her very wet hair.

She washed and ran a comb through the tangled mess on her head. After she felt somewhat settled she walked back to the office. The kid stood, hands on his hips, looking at the Jag.

"Damn, Ma'am. Those aren't bullet holes? What the hell happened?" She still wasn't sure herself.

"Did you call the sheriff?" She was calm now.

"Yes Ma'am. And I mentioned the bullet holes."

The sheriff showed up in less than five minutes, his lights flashing and siren screaming, just as the rain stopped. O'Mara described what had happened—a vague but truthful story about wanting to see some south county scenery. Was caught up watching the rain front slide down the mountains when all the shooting started. The only small items she left out were the reason why she was there and her pistol hidden in her purse.

She moved the Jag into the garage for the boy to clean up, while she and the sheriff drove to where she thought the shooting occurred. "Sparks" was the name he gave—she couldn't tell if was a last name, first, or nickname. It was difficult to find the spot in the fading sunlight. The rain had obliterated any tracks. They left after ten minutes.

The kid at the station had done a better job than she could have expected. The glass was gone and he'd managed to rig a plastic sheet to cover the rear window. Six bullet holes, three to port and three to starboard, were the size of dimes. He found her cell phone under the seat. She was glad she'd slid the Beretta into her purse—if the kid had found it, there'd be more than a few more questions, questions very difficult to answer. The sheriff finished his interview, they exchanged cards, he told her to drive careful-like, and left. O'Mara sat in the office another thirty minutes, warmed up, dried off a bit, drank a cup of weak but hot coffee, and thanked the kid with two twenties. The ride home to Walnut Creek took forever.

4a

O'Mara wasted a lot of precious water in the shower. It took almost an hour to wash away the blood and fear. "What the hell's going on?" she asked over and over. Basil stood guard at the bathroom door.

She'd talked to Bryan on the drive home. He said he'd meet her at her house. No, she'd be fine. He was as confused as anyone about the shooting. It was becoming crystal clear the shooting in the BART lot was more than a simple carjacking gone bad—deadly more.

Bryan said he would be over early the next morning, no excuses. She called the office—only one message, from the live Franklin regarding her check and when she could expect it. "Damn her," she glared at the dashboard. "I almost became room temperature this afternoon and all she wants is her fucking money. Well, screw her."

Two three-finger scotches helped soften the shock and pain. She took stock of where she was in this craziness—the Jag was okay except for the added ventilation which Reginald would fix. The cut on her forehead would barely be a scar in a week. Both the cell phone and the Beretta needed cleaning. Maybe a few hours at the range wouldn't be a bad idea either—and it might also take the edge off her jitters. And lastly, her she needed to replace her favorite blouse; silk didn't travel well through gravel and mud.

Basil nuzzled her arm. The big lovable mutt had an unbelievable crush on her—as a couple of dates found out when they got a little too forward. He was always there with his *basso profundo* bark when needed and made a good pillow some nights. If only guys were as nice as Basil she wouldn't still be single. Besides, who'd marry a girl whose job description included ducking bullets? Basil just loved her for her money.

The telephone rang. Ross Clayburn was shocked over what had happened. Sheriff Sparks—last name she noted—was a friend of his, had called him about the shooting. Clayburn wanted to know everything. She told him what happened, especially the sudden appearance of the truck. No, she couldn't describe the exact color because of the rain, dark green or black—had no explanation or even a guess. He would talk to his security people in the morning and get back to her. Had she seen them, they drove a white pickup? No? She thanked him for his concern and hung up.

"Well Basil, what do you think? Does he know what's going on, or was he truly surprised? For now I'll go with surprised, with reservations." She looked out the window onto the patio. The scotch glass was wet, leaving a ring on the table every time she lifted it. Six or eight rings, if anyone was counting. "Damn it, of course. Why didn't I see it earlier? If they wanted to kill me, they would have. Three shots from a rifle three inches apart from at least 200 yards—that means a scope and a very accurate shot. They wanted to scare me, not make you an orphan. That's why they took off when they got too close. Of course they didn't want me to see them. Strange, very strange." She poured another three-fingers and added another ring on the table.

4b

The doorbell rang promptly at 9:00. Basil barked deeply and ran to the door. Though O'Mara had been up for hours, she was, even now, still a little foggy. Too little food, a little too much Red Label, not enough sleep. The bell rang again. She recognized the tall silhouette of Kevin Bryan through the curtain and glass. She handed him a cup of coffee as he walked through the doorway.

"Good morning. You look like four rounds with Tyson, my love," he said, studying the bandage on her forehead.

"Same to you and the horse you came in on." She turned

her back and padded down the wood floor in her bare feet toward the kitchen. Bryan followed her soft moves with his eyes. He liked her bounce, smiled as she turned her profile into the streaming sunlight.

"The place looks great. Hi-ya Basil, how's it hanging?" Basil rubbed his muzzle against Kevin's hand and together they followed O'Mara into the kitchen. "Sharon, it does look great. My place is such a dump. When can you give me a hand getting it to look right?"

"When you finally have some money. Get your ex married so you can free up some of that cash for yourself." O'Mara had only met the ex Mrs. Bryan once, years ago, and to this day couldn't figure out why Kevin had married her. *To each their own poison.*

"You okay?" he asked, blowing on his coffee.

"Yeah, I'm fine. I've been over and over all of this and I still can't get a handle on it. The briefcase, the murders, the shooting at me and now to cap it all off I've got Franklin whining at me about the money. It's a son of a bitch."

She slid a chair out from the kitchen table and sat down. The coffee mug warmed her hands. The TV on the counter was on, the never-ending news muted. She glanced up to see Ross Clayburn in formal wear waltzing into an official looking building with other equally well dressed people. She hit the sound, ". . . local dignitaries and VIPs" the voice-over reported, "attended last night's five hundred dollar a plate fund raiser for Herman Pell's reelection for Santa Clara county supervisor. Supervisor Pell has long been a booster for Santa Clara County businesses and public causes. He's facing a tough battle from no-growth advocates and the Green Ridges Intelligent Protection Electorate during this upcoming campaign. The number of heavy hitters attending this fundraiser attests to his popularity among builders and developers. Unfortunately, Supervisor Pell's wife couldn't attend. She's been ill." The program broke for a commercial.

"What was that?" Bryan asked.

"The first guy, with the gray hair and mustache, was Mr. Ross Clayburn, the owner of the shooting range I was at yesterday. Let me show you." With two clicks on the remote she backed up the broadcast to show Clayburn in his tux.

"How'd you do that?"

"What?"

"Back it up, how the hell did you do that?"

She looked at him like he was a Martian. "Easy, all you do is hit this and then this and it will play back any show you're watching. Cool for sports."

"I have to get one of those things. Since they dropped the old signal, all I get is crap, but then all I got was crap before, so what's the difference."

"You're so twentieth century. Anyway, Clayburn called last night—maybe even during that fundraiser—to offer his concern and help. I thanked him and hung up. He's certainly on top of things."

"Interesting series of coincidences building up around Mr. Clayburn," Kevin said. "If Santa Clara is similar to our county, all growth and development in their jurisdiction must be approved by the Board of Supervisors—especially if it involves the Sphere of Influence Zone of cities within the county. Having Mr. Pell on your side would be a great asset, considering the rabble the GRIPE people can muster."

"GRIPE?"

"Green Ridges Intelligent Protection Electorate or something like it. A wacky group if there ever was one—with a grammatically challenged name."

"How would they be involved?"

"For properties to change zoning, plans and documents must be submitted to the county for review to see if they conform to the current General Plan. If not, the General Plan must first be modified. The submitted plan is reviewed for environmental impacts—you know; things like traffic, sewer, water, costs to the county, impacts to ground squirrels, snakes and other creepy things before it's approved. This report is then voted on, for acceptability, by the County Planning Commission and the Supervisors. If approved, the plan can then be used for drawing up tentative maps and final subdivision maps. The property's then vested with new rights—which can change its value. We're talking a lot of money, ten times, even a hundred times the original agricultural value. The longer this process goes on, the more expensive it can be. The more expensive the dirt, the more buyers pay for houses and things. Green Ridges tries to slow or halt these projects by bringing into the game—and it's a game—things that will incite their followers into protesting the development. I don't know—it seems a silly process, accomplishes little, and eventually corrupts everyone involved. It puts money and power together—two of the three great human weaknesses. This affects everyone involved: developers, politicians and environmentalists. Sometimes I think I understand the developers more, since money and buildings are tangibles. The politicians and environmentalists I don't understand—except the power to control people can be even more intoxicating than money."

"Where the hell did you learn all that?" Sharon's eyes were glazed over. She looked fondly at the empty scotch glass still sitting on the counter.

"A neighbor of mine is a city planner. It only takes a few drinks to get him going on and on about the idiots who run the government and county offices. I started watching things, even took in a couple of Supervisor's hearings when I was out at the courthouse. After sitting through some of those meetings, he may be right. It's frightening how people who don't build can control how and where we live. Very frightening—but oh hell, it's too early to be so serious."

"No kidding. What about the briefcase?"

"Nothing more then what I told you yesterday. No prints, even on the locks, not even a partial. Very nicely cleaned up—and I do mean cleaned up. Didn't even find any of Franklin's prints except on his credit cards. The CalTrans fellow left his prints all over the outside but that's understandable. Mrs. Franklin didn't anything in the box that had any connection or bearing on the case—just bonds, deeds and insurance information. She was surprised to find seventy-five Krugerrands. She didn't realize he was buying gold. No leads beyond what we already have."

She poured more coffee. "Could you have your guys go over the Jaguar? The shooter left three nice holes in the side and blew out the rear window. One may be stuck in the seat. I'm certain they were only trying to scare me off. The spread was too close to be misses. He knew how to shoot. If he wanted me dead, I would be."

She stood up. "What really pisses me off is the way my car was trashed. Took me a year to get it painted, the interior fixed and finally find a good mechanic. Now I need a new rear window, patching and filling on the doors, repairs to the upholstery. Damn! It was almost like he enjoyed doing it."

"At least you're alive to enjoy all of those nice activities you have to do now. I could have been over here this morning trying to explain to Basil why he's coming home to live with me." Bryan looked into her face and smiled. She knew he really cared for her.

"What's on your list today?" he asked.

"I've got to go back into the office. In two days in a row, can't stand it. I have to try to resolve Franklin's check and then do a little investigating down south. Maybe talk to GRIPE. That what you called it? The comment on the TV made me curious about what their concern is for this property. Also, see if Herman Pell has any information about Clayburn's development—Clayburn has obviously contributed to his campaign, so I'm interested in what influence his money has purchased."

"After the check is sent to Franklin, why stay with this?" He knew quite well why—no one tries to kill Sharon O'Mara without getting her seriously upset. "So you think there's still a connection between Franklin and Clayburn?"

"Yes I do, kind of a gut feeling, but tangible. Clayburn and Cimoni called the outline fraudulent, but it was very close to the details on the colored plan they gave me. That's surprising, considering how he reacted to my comments about the outline. The deed in Franklin's jacket was for a parcel of land across the street from where I was shot at. It wasn't included in the plan area. The coincidence is too great to blow it off like they did."

Basil pushed up against her leg. She passed him some cold toast. He didn't mind.

4c

After Bryan left, O'Mara showered for the fourth time in two days, counted bruises and cuts, rubbed lotion on old scars, dressed in soft cottons and tennis shoes, and, making sure everything was in order in the house, and after telling Basil she would be back in a few hours, she drove the car over to Reginald's who, after seeing the damage, almost broke into tears.

"What have you done to my car," he demanded, in an Americanized version of Cockney. "How can you treat this car this way?"

"It wasn't my doing, Reggie. There I was minding my own business, parked in a field when someone started shooting holes in it. If he was also trying to hit me, he was a lousy shot—kept hitting the car. In either event, the car got the brunt of the damage. I got away with only a nick."

It was only then Reggie noticed the bandage on her forehead. "You okay?" he asked softly, the mechanic's edge out of his voice.

"Yeah, I'm fine. Can we get her fixed?"

"This is bloody Reginald you're asking, dearie. The holes and the window can be fixed, of course. I still have some paint left from the boot repair. The windscreen may take a few days to locate. There's a yard in Oakland that may have a spare. But I can get started on the holes this afternoon. None of that Bondo either—solder and a patch. That's what I'll do." He was proud of his work and it showed as she looked around the small shop. Two old Bentley's—one black, the other silver, and a forty-year old green MGB-GT were parked in formation along the wall. An Austin Healy 100M seemed caught in the middle of an autopsy—the parts laid out on tables that surrounded the carcass, the frame on blocks, windshields removed.

"Is there a place around here where I can rent a car?"

"Up Main two blocks and make a right. One of those national chains; never can remember the name. They have all the usual crap. Normally I'd lend you my old Vauxhall, but it's with the owner of that silver Bentley for a couple of days. Sorry. He begged to have the chance to drive it."

"That's okay Reggie, I'll see what I can find." She pulled her handbag from the car and headed up Main Street.

Downtown Walnut Creek had been buffeted by change for years—some for the good, some for the bad. Good things were: better shops and retail stores, new trees and benches, more parking, and more tablecloth restaurants. An obvious sign was higher end cars and SUVs parked along the curbs. However on the down side, it had lost some great little shops too—the family owned bakery folded when higher rent got them, the thrift shops with great old shirts she liked to frequent were whittled down to just a few, the owner owned and operated restaurants that remained were just a handful. The village had grown up, but in many ways was still staying small. She wondered how long that would last.

The rental was one of those cute underpowered Japanese models that got millions of miles to the gallon, had all the gimmicks and do-dads, and the personality of a toaster. Cute color, especially if you're having a gender crisis. A bout of clinical depression was developing over the state of her beloved Jaguar.

5a

Two days later Sharon O'Mara tried to set up a meeting with County Supervisor Herman Pell. After a long hold, Pell took the phone and told her he wouldn't be available until the following week. His schedule wouldn't permit it; he's a busy man; meetings here, fundraisers there, busy, busy.

So busy. Why was he was trying to avoid her, someone he'd never met?

It was something she said during their telephone conversation, the part about the Clayburn Company and a murder, which gave Pell pause. He waited a few beats, again said he was very sorry, and offered he could only meet late next week, at the earliest. "Call my secretary," and hung up.

Mrs. Franklin's one million dollar check was finally released. O'Mara happened to hear via a client of Reginald's the house in Lafayette was for sale and Anne Franklin was moving to the desert. Luckily, she didn't have to deliver the check—or she might have said something she would not regret.

With the investigation by the company officially closed, O'Mara was assigned to another case that involved a damaged child, playground equipment, a homeowners association, and a schnauzer. It held her interest for all of the time it took to hear about it from her supervisor. She left the office with a stack of paperwork considerably thicker than the Franklin case. Children, dogs, and HOA's do that. Sitting in the rented Japanese version of heaven on wheels, she lowered the automatic windows—the back ones only went half-way—pulled the Marlboro's from her bag, lit one, took a deep breath, and waited for the smoke alarm to go off. Hearing none, she tried to reconstruct the puzzle from the pieces left strewn about.

It was now extremely personal. She'd been lied to, that she was certain of. And shot at, the Jaguar confirmed that. Since her days in Baghdad, she took someone's effort to kill her as personal. Her lieutenant's rank in Army Military Police made her a target in the chaotic days in the first year of the war. After they took the city, an uneasy calm followed; a calm that camouflaged the real terror the next five years would become when nobody or anything could be trusted. It steeled her to insure the safety of both her platoon and herself.

Being caught in the open by the sniper unleashed all the memories of the war. She'd never had flashbacks or paranoid attacks since the day she left the service. She knew deep in her soul these experiences were a part of her. In the past they'd helped her in difficult and deadly situations. This time she'd been blind-sided. Now she was pissed. Why had she become a target? Who did the shooting? What was the reason or reasons behind it? She wasn't sure what she would do when she found the answer, but one thing was certain—next time it would be a fairer fight.

Two critical points stood out. First, only a few people knew she was going to the property that afternoon. Second, one of those people called to see how she was. That certainly wasn't anything she could take to the sheriff, especially since he so dutifully reported to Clayburn after the attack. Her interest lay in the greater *Why*. If Clayburn was involved, why jeopardize the whole scheme over a harmless visit? If he wasn't involved, who wanted her to drop the whole affair and leave it alone? And besides, what could be going on that required such extreme action to discourage her from seeing the property? One slip in the mud and she would have added to the body count in this story and that was something she wouldn't have enjoyed.

Bryan had called before she left for the office to let her know the other thug finally was well enough to be questioned. The kid knew nothing about the briefcase, never saw it. He vaguely remembered someone had pushed him out of the way against the dashboard just after the air bags exploded, some fumbling of hands around his feet before he passed out. He didn't remember any gunshots or seeing anyone.

The kid had a juvenile record that went back at least seven years—the usual family angst of drugs, no father, dysfunctional mother, and some loose gang connections. He gave up the driver hoping to cop a lighter sentence—he'd be lucky to serve just twenty-five years. The carjacking was an attempt to bribe their way into a Berkeley gang. The kid was seventeen, the dead driver eighteen.

"There was someone else?"

"Looks like it. Whoever it was first checked the front seat after they shot the kid, then pulled the rear door open, and took the briefcase. Must have worn gloves. Later they removed what they wanted, cleaned the case, and dumped it. He may also be the guy who shot the kid and maybe Franklin. They both had .357 holes in them. The driver had a chrome .357 revolver, one bullet fire."

"Yeah, that's what I'm beginning to think. And one more point, he must have had a car or something else to leave the BART lot—the case didn't get to the side of the freeway by itself. Maybe he took the train to another station, and then dumped the case. You checked the cabs?"

"Yup. No one left in a cab after Franklin's train arrived. All the companies that use the station were out. The rain had them all on runs—there were none at the stand."

"Okay, on another matter, loosely connected. I tried to get a meeting with Pell—too busy, maybe next week. Touched a nerve when I said "Clayburn." There's something these people know and they aren't talking. My next stop is the county planning office. Maybe somebody down there can clue me in. I've got a date with one of the planners at three this afternoon. I'll let you know what happens."

"Call me later and let me know how it goes. I'm getting jealous already."

5b

The traffic to the Santa Clara County Planning office was easy—one rear-ender in Milpitas. A small car and a gasoline tanker had mixed it up. The delay and detour only added twenty-five minutes. The smoke from the accident could be seen for miles. She actually arrived early for her appointment.

Jim Rodriguez, Senior Planner, introduced himself and directed her to a small conference room. A large aerial photo covered one wall.

"Thank you for seeing me, I know you must be busy," she started.

"Yeah, very busy. The staff cutbacks only reduced staff, not the work. I'm carrying the load of two senior planners. In the old days—three short years ago—fees were coming in at a rate that allowed us the luxury of enough staff to handle the mundane, day-to-day stuff. Now, no permits plus no fees equals no staff budget. We double up. I just wish the salary went up with the workload. The usual bureaucratic lament, right?"

"I work for a large insurance company. I know bureaucracy—it's even in the private sector," she replied as she scanned the photo. "Is this where Clayburn Company's properties are?" Her finger tapped the lowest left center portion of the photo.

"Yes, that's about where they plan the entry to the project. It's a strong location—good access and it's in the center of the property. They also control all four corners and the two corners at the next exit south. They have a good grip on future commercial and office sites visible from the freeway. That's worth a lot. It will create quite an impact on regional traffic volumes—which is part of our concern."

"I met with Clayburn last week and he gave this to me." She held out the torn plan. "Is this similar to the plan they've submitted?" Rodriguez took the mud smeared plan. He walked up to the photo, looked at the plan, then the aerial.

"Ms. O'Mara, I haven't seen this particular map before, but it's pretty similar to the plans they submitted. You have to understand this process is an evolution. They submit, we comment, they revise, we comment, they submit again, we comment again then schedule meetings, never ending meetings it seems. Often this process seems to go on forever. They think we don't care. We think they're trying to pull a fast one. It's all a game, but a serious one. We're both trying to achieve something, a quality community." He sat down at the table and she pulled up a chair across from him.

"This is our bible." He held up a thick spiral bound book. "The county's General Plan. This book was created at extreme expense to guide the county through a process like this. It sets up goals, policies and actions that determine how the county will grow, where things will go and how we assess submitted projects. It's supposed to help, but it only complicates an already complicated process."

"What happens when the submission doesn't conform to the General Plan?"

"The property's existing designation must be amended. This adds a bit more complexity to the process but the procedures are all outlined in the General Plan. For large plans like this," he pointed to the drawing, "we also require a Specific Plan. It details densities, land uses, environmental impacts, noise, and fiscal implementation. If it's approved, the Specific Plan is melded into the General Plan. It becomes the overriding document for the community, but it's not all. The county will also require an Environmental Impact Report. It's an independent assessment. It compares the plan to its impacts and presents these impacts for an open review by the County. The final decision is made by the Board of Supervisors; they determine what's acceptable based on the findings."

"Is there much opposition?" She was studying the stand of trees where the shooter must have hidden.

"Today everything has opponents—some well founded, others not. It's not our place as staff planners to take sides. This project has major muscle against it. Primarily a coalition centered on environmentalist David Schenk, president of GRIPE. They've come out strongly against this project, primarily due to the impact on traffic, pollution, and loss of wetlands. That's the Holy Trinity for most developmental protests. All you have to do is mention any of these three to bring other anti-development groups to join your march, whatever the project."

"We try very hard not to allow these groups to influence us," he continued, "but it's tough—especially with younger staff members. Guys like Schenk speak quite eloquently about the end of culture and life as we know it—and they lay it at the feet of the developers, blame all the evils of society on them and their camp followers. Unfortunately, most of this isn't the fault of the developer. It is all those Easterners fleeing cold winters, immigrants fleeing their homebred evils and good native Californians begetting more Californians. They need homes, jobs, schools, stores, parks, open space, trees, birds, fish and the grandest quality of life anywhere on the planet. The builders try to provide it, we try to manage it and the politicians—whether elected like the Board or self-appointed like Schenk—try to screw it up. Don't quote me on that, Ms. O'Mara." He looked directly at her and cracked a smile.

"I don't envy your job as referee. This guy Schenk, is he local?"

"Kind of. He's from up around Berkeley somewhere. I sat on a couple of regional committees with him. Sharp guy, always organizing, knows his stuff. People tell me he's a Rhodes Scholar or something. Spent some time with Greenpeace on a ship in the north Pacific, a whale thing. He isn't into hiding his agenda, everyone knows where he stands and why. He wants power and his organization provides the forum he needs to exert it. He's at his best in front of a hometown crowd. They hang on to his every word. He doesn't miss much at hearings. He's a fast learner with an incredible temper he tries to control. I think when the time is right he'll run for office—local or even state, or maybe an influential job with a congressman or senator."

"Or maybe control those who do run for office?" she predicted.

"Yeah, you may be right. Politicians are still at the mercy of their constituents, whether rich builders, manufacturers or organized environmental and social movements. All we want are good plans and communities. Sadly, sometimes compromise cuts the heart out of development." He turned and looked at the map.

"Did you hear that when I was on the property last week someone shot at me? Three rounds in the side of my car, one through my rear windshield. Someone didn't want me to check on what's happening out there."

"You're kidding. Do the police know?" His job was routine, even boring—this revelation brightened his day.

"Yes, I went out there later with Sheriff Sparks. We couldn't find much though. He took my statement and after I left he immediately reported to Clayburn."

"That's no surprise—the sheriff owes his campaign coffers and reelection to Clayburn. Being sheriff is a good job. Being reelected is icing on the cake. He's a good guy though, and pretty honest. In fact he fired one of his men for getting a little carried away with an arrest that broke a few ribs. Sparks gave him an hour to clear out his things and the Board supported him even when the guy sued. The County won—the guy got nothing. Yes, Sparks is an okay guy from my perspective; though I'm surprised he answered the call. Even the sheriff is cutting staff."

"There's a Planning Commission meeting next Tuesday," Rodriguez continued. "You should attend. We're going to discuss the general aspects of the project. The following week we'll have a joint workshop between the Planning Commission and the Board of Supervisors. There will be time then for the public to speak. Schenk will be there, the fellow Cimoni from Clayburn. Do you know him? Should be some good fireworks."

"Yeah, I know Cimoni. Does the name Richard Franklin ring any bells?"

Rodriguez stared at her for a moment. "Doesn't ring a bell, at least in any planning context. I know a Franklin from school days, but I'm sure you're not talking about him."

"No, I don't think so. This Franklin was about sixty. Shot in a carjacking a few weeks back."

"Dead?"

"Yes, very messy."

"Why are you asking?"

"No particular reason other than he was a client with a re-mote possibility of a connection to this development. But most of the roads I've gone down lead to mud holes." She turned again to the wall photo and paused. "You've been a great help, thanks a lot. If I have any questions, can I call?"

"Absolutely, you have my card and my email. Anytime."

She stood up and shook his hand—strong and firm, just the right pressure. As bureaucrats go, this one was all right.

"Thanks again for your time."

5c

O'Mara needed to feel the site through her feet, and this time wear the right boots. She didn't call Clayburn for permission and she told Bryan where she'd be in case she was not welcome a second time. She tromped the roads and side streets, trying to imagine how the community would fill the valley. Some of the creeks would remain. The trees and woods tidied into parks free of poison oak and barbed wire. Office buildings would buf-fer housing against freeway noise. She stood in the village cen-ter, seeing how the parks would be connected with trails and greenways to all the residential neighborhoods. Rodriguez was right—it was a plan with merit and thought. Why kill people to have it stopped? She only saw one of Clayburn's top-notch security people asleep in his truck under some trees. She walked through the grove where the sharpshooter had been setup, but there were no shell casings lying about. He must have policed them or kept them in the truck.

The area north of the site, the land within San Jose city lim-its, was full of homes and businesses. The tops of the high tech buildings etched fantastic shapes along the ridge that separated the valley from the spread of the Bay Area. Growth was a con-stant. Who was it who said, "If you stop growing, you'll die." She couldn't remember, but some of the feelings of the environ-mentalists were valid. This was a pretty valley full of orchards and trees, creeks and fields, but then again so was Silicon Valley less than thirty years ago. Maybe Rodriguez was right—it would be nice to stop and take a breather. Unfortunately no one else seems to want to.

She stopped to see the kid at the gas station. He wasn't impressed with her rental and said so. He liked her Jag, though the flow-through ventilation was a little extreme for him. He was glad to know she was okay. O'Mara headed north.

She reported to Bryan. "Nothing new. Rodriguez, the planner, helped clear up a few of the issues about the property, but he didn't have any reason to believe they were worth shooting people over. This guy Schenk with Green Ridges is interesting though—environmental organizer and activist with a power-tripping ego. Seems to hold the environmental groups in the valley together."

"Franklin?"

"Nothing new. The planner never mentioned his name and when I asked, never heard of him."

"This whole Franklin thing might be a dead end," Kevin said. "Maybe there's simply no connection."

"But what about those papers? They're not something just anyone would have. And when Clayburn's people saw them, they seemed genuinely amazed Franklin would have them. In fact, I'll bet there were more of those papers in his briefcase, and after the shootings they were less than skillfully removed."

There was a silence on the other end for a few seconds before Bryan responded. "You may be very right. If you put the few facts we have together, that's a logical conclusion. Are you thinking Franklin was trying to set up a blackmail scheme and those papers were going to be the bait?"

"It's possible. Maybe he stole the documents or had someone steal them from Clayburn's office. I tend to lean to the latter though—the security is pretty good around Clayburn's office so it would be very hard to get in there as an outsider. Maybe someone passed him the documents that night. He put a couple in his jacket, and then was followed when he went down to BART. Maybe someone hired those thugs to steal the briefcase. And maybe they got carried away or saw the car as an opportunity not to miss. Maybe the real shooter was watching to make sure nothing went wrong—and when it did, shot Franklin or at least tried to. And then maybe when the kids took off and crashed, he figured he wouldn't have to pay if there were no witnesses." She noticed her speedometer and slowed. This Japanese thing still could go fast and was a lot quieter than her injured partner.

"Very interesting theory, Investigator O'Mara. And it almost works. But who would be that concerned about those papers or the damage they could do? Blackmail seems kind of petty for a group of Clayburn's caliber. He would simply pay off and expense it no differently than the politicians he supports. And Franklin's wealth and background certainly doesn't support the notion he was a shakedown expert. He didn't need the dough and the papers he had were minor. It also assume guys like Clayburn and Cimoni wouldn't be so careless with their big bribes or promotional expenses. They know arrogance will always get you in the end."

O'Mara thought about it for a moment. "I think I'm at least part right. Now I have to figure out which part."

"I really think you should drop this whole deal. Someone is out there looking for you now, someone who could have cared less about you three weeks ago. But someone now thinks you know more than you really do and that someone maybe wants you dead. And besides I would rather have you as my roommate than your dog."

"Getting kind of serious now, aren't we?" She swerved between two semis hauling shipping containers.

"Yes damn it, I am. And like I said I don't need a dog at this time of my life. I prefer to visit him at your place. Call me later when you've a chance."

Sharon flipped the cell closed and laid it on the seat next to her. The radio was playing an Ellington piece from some obscure jazz station on the Peninsula. She remembered sadly that it was the last of the great jazz stations left in the Bay Area. The ride home was melancholy.

6a

Pell had told her, "...tomorrow morning at 7:30 at Jake's Coffee Shop on First Street. We can talk there."

She was early, no traffic. Pell was a bit pudgy with a touch of pre-coffee puffiness about his eyes. He came in alone and sat across from the only woman in the place and he assumed who she was.

"Ms. O'Mara, Herman Pell." He extended his hand.

"Mr. Pell, thank you for seeing me." She returned the classic politician's handshake.

"What's this all about? The sheriff told me you were shot at last week on the Clayburn property. Why didn't you say so when we talked? Is that why you're here?" O'Mara quickly assessed this guy as intense, too intense, sweat started to bead on his forehead.

"No, even though that's a good lead in. I'm surprised Clayburn didn't mention it that night, you know, the night of the fundraiser. Did Sparks discover anything more?"

"No, Clayburn didn't say anything, and no, Sparks didn't even find a shell casing. He had two of his deputies walk the area, but they came up with nothing. Why were you out there—you're not in real estate? He told me you're an insurance investigator, so what's your interest in Clayburn's land?"

The fact that he brought up Clayburn in his opening didn't go unnoticed by O'Mara. His style was confrontational and questioning, not the best way to start a conversation with her.

"Mr. Pell, no one shoots at me and waltzes off unscathed." Her tone was matter of fact. "Whoever it is will slip up and I'll be there to get him. However, the reason I'm here is to find out your connection to Ross Clayburn and Allen Cimoni. Both of them are contributors to your reelection campaign, yes?"

"Why the hell should I tell you?" he snapped, a very small bead of sweat sat on the tip of his nose, wishing to fall.

"Because it's in your interest to maintain your distance. Two people have died and there may be connections to Clayburn. Of course this is all unofficial—I'm only speculating." She looked directly at him and smiled.

"What are you implying? I've asked Mr. Clayburn for his help with a number of civic events and issues. He's been generous his time and his money. He loves this community, has helped it in many ways, and yes, both of them have contributed to my reelection. So what's your problem?" The sweat drop fell from his nose and hit the Formica with a soundless splat.

"No problem. I'm not implying anything, just stating the facts. Clayburn needs your vote for his community plan to be approved. You need dollars for reelection. You know the old phrase—scratch my back and I'll scratch yours." She took a sip of her coffee.

"So?"

"So I would caution you, that's all. This is personal, Mr. Pell. It has nothing to do with my job or directly with the deaths. I don't like being shot at. I'm not into extreme sports."

"Well I'm sorry. I may eventually even be sorry they were such bad marksmen. I may even be sorry for Mr. Clayburn, but I do know you should mind your own goddamn business and stay out of my county. Good morning Ms. O'Mara." He stood up and looked toward the door.

"Thank you, Mr. Pell. I hope your reelection goes smoothly and your wife is better."

He looked back at her with a defiant yet somewhat pained look. On the way out he stopped to shake the hands of three suits in the front booth and wink at the waitress.

O'Mara knew he knew more, a lot more. Clayburn's connections were too deep to deny. If she heard from Clayburn during the next twelve hours, she would know Pell was hooked and hooked deep. He wouldn't be able to shake himself free.

Her next call was to David Schenk. Rodriguez's comments interested her. What made him tick and why? He would be glad to meet her at 10:00 at his office in downtown San Jose.

6b

The weather was warming, and, by the calendar, spring would arrive in just a few weeks; the late winter rains had washed San Jose clean and bright. Even the empty lots along the downtown streets were lush with weeds growing through the cracks in the worn asphalt.

Like all of California, San Jose had irrevocably changed. Silicon Valley had spread south through San Jose like a virus. Silicon Valley, really more a state of mind and economics than geography, ran from San Mateo to San Martin along the backbone of the old King's Highway, El Camino Real—now sadly and inadequately renamed Highway 101. Along the banks of its river of traffic, land values had tripled and then tripled again— and probably would multiply again sometime in the future. Silicon Valley economics permitted some to stay and forced others to leave. The old timers, those who'd planted the straight rows of orchards and grape vines, were the first to leave, turning their land over for a final crop—winding rows of houses. Those who took possession paid handsomely for the privilege. The valley and the people who lived and worked there were as confusing as those that sometimes called it Silicone Valley—in many ways it was just as fake.

GRIPE's offices were in a politically correct older building in a mature part of San Jose. O'Mara climbed one flight and hung a left. She wondered how Schenk's handicapped supporters could get to these offices—no elevator retrofit. The receptionist was a Chinese-American girl. She smiled hearing O'Mara's name, and retreated down a darkened hall toward an open door.

Posters and artwork papered the walls and tabletops, not one man or man-made thing could be seen in any of the images. It was like man and nature couldn't co-exist. She turned at the sound of heavy boots on the hardwood. "Good morning Ms. O'Mara, I'm David Schenk." He provided a strong handshake.

"What can we do for you? Your call was vague, but it did get my interest up. Are you involved with Clayburn on his land in the southern part of the county?" He led her past a series of cubicles. "My humble office." He pointed to a doorway. "We have two here in the Bay Area, our home office is up in Berkeley. This one is our war center for our work in the South Bay. Makes for rough travel for me, but it supports our members and affiliates down here."

"I'm not involved directly with Clayburn,' Sharon answered. "In fact, I'm with Professional Life and looking into some insurance issues that may link to Clayburn. A client of our company was killed. We're trying to clarify how involved he may have been in a Clayburn project. I thought our dead client may have been involved with your group." She took the coffee he offered. They sat on the worn couch under the window. She wondered if the rich Colombian taste was politically correct.

"Who was this person?"

O'Mara briefly told him the story of the killing and the information they'd uncovered. She mentioned the shooting of her car and some of the discussions since. She didn't tell him about her meeting with Pell earlier in the morning.

"I'm very sorry those people died, but I don't know anyone with that name. Richard Franklin, right? Such a shame."

O'Mara took another sip, "Sorry to hear that, I was hoping for some connection, tie up the loose ends."

"I understand, but sorry."

She looked at the large poster behind Schenk, a large bear with a salmon in its mouth.

"Why are you opposed to the plan they've put together? It seems very thorough and complete. It looks like a wonderful place to live—open space, parks and schools near to the homes, jobs and shopping right there. What's the problem?"

"You're interested in this project for other reasons?" He set his cup on a pile of papers.

"Indirectly, yes."

"I'm fighting for what we may lose forever. One more piece of open land would be lost. Land that can buffer developers' greedy urban expansion—sprawl if you will. If this project moves forward, there's less reason to in-fill areas closer to the city core where facilities already exist, things like utilities, transit, and other county services. I'm fighting to insure that what is built will not cost taxpayers more than it produces in revenues. Green Ridges stands against projects that don't have affordable housing, against projects marketed to a very select group of people."

"Are you suggesting there are racial implications in the plan? I find that hard to accept."

"I'm not saying anything specific—only that these communities tend to be homogeneous, of limited racial and economic mix. If this implies racial segregation, I'm only stating the facts." He raised both his hands and turned them in an uplifting motion. O'Mara saw a religious implication in the gesture.

"So besides a strong environmental concern, you have a social and political point of view as well? How can you and your organization be so righteous?" She studied his face to see what might be hidden within his answer.

"We are here to be a sounding board for the community. There are many groups," he stood and began to pace the small room, "that need me to manage and direct their efforts. Efforts that alone don't have the strength to change policy or educate politicians and stakeholders. I help these groups to act together in a collective way, for their common reasons. However diverse they are, united in a common front. It's very difficult for the media or politicians to ignore us. My role is to place their concerns before the people in a public forum. This is how we can make the greatest impact. A little noise gets the press excited, and this excitement translates into information and eventually better legislation." He emphasized the last phrase with a clenched fist.

"Do you ever support growth?"

"Our organization never endorses a particular builder or community plan. This would compromise our ability to hold neutral ground. Ground that permits us to challenge and question both public and private impacts to the environment. Take Clayburn's proposed development to the south. Yes Ms. O'Mara, it's a complete community, at least on paper. Has it all, but isn't it really just a way for white people to escape the blacks and browns of San Jose. Isn't it a way to shut them out of their future? If the Board listens only to people like Clayburn, they won't listen to the people, the people who need quality afford-able homes close to their jobs. People who can't afford a decent car where there are no transit alternatives. If the community supports this continuing sprawl, there won't be the resources needed to fix and improve those parts of the community that need help." He looked at her for some form of approval. She shook her head.

She had heard this spiel before, the finite pie argument. There was only so much and if someone took more than their "fair" share there was less left to redistribute. The argument was simplistic. The factual point was that communities like this cre-ated more value than the public costs required to build them. These newly created values were in jobs and increases in land values. The pie could be multiplied, more pies made, allowing more people to share the pies, more and better places for people to live.

"What's your opinion of Councilman Pell?"

"Pell's a stooge. He's always been in the pocket of the devel-opment community. His campaign is financed by them and he has supported their actions for years. The county has suffered because San Jose has gotten too strong. There isn't the despera-tion in the county like I've seen in the city. The county doesn't seem to care what its impact is on San Jose. That's why we're taking both of them, Clayburn and Pell, head on."

"Is there some form of middle ground?"

He laughed. "You sound like a matchmaker, one of those ladies who tries to find wives or husbands for someone, always negotiating. Always asking questions like: 'Is there some middle ground here?' Ms. O'Mara, there may always be a middle ground. My goal is to always occupy that middle ground—and from a position of strength. My supporters demand nothing less than victory. Compromise is a tough place to live."

"I may just show up at the hearings then—ought to be pretty interesting, kind of like a prize fight. Only the winner never leaves the ring."

"Good analogy. A prizefighter never underestimates his opponent. I can assure you I don't either. The hearings will be very interesting."

Sensing the conversation wasn't going to go much further, she stood. "Well, Mr. Schenk, thank you. I wish I could offer you good luck, but my sympathies, though not with Clayburn, are not behind you either. My sympathies fall back to Richard Franklin. Unfortunately those sympathies will not help him a bit. Again, thank you."

"If there's anything else you need, please contact me. Thanks for stopping by." He walked her to the door of his office.

As she walked down the corridor to the stairs, she could understand why some people follow men like that. They're strong and positive, charismatic, rabble-rousers and leaders—and dangerous. They provide direction to lost people and to habitual followers. Others with his personality would steal little old ladies' pensions without a second thought. She walked out of the dark stair well into the bright spring sun and toward the androgynous Japanese rental.

6c

Two messages waited for her. The first was Bryan checking in. How's she doing? How did her meeting with Pell go? The second was from Clayburn asking her to lunch. He'd heard she was in San Jose and was wondering if she were free at 1:00. He left his cell number.

"Now I wonder how he knew I was in San Jose?" She laughed out loud. Pell didn't waste any time calling his puppet master.

"Ross Clayburn here." His voice was crisp and to the point.

"Mr. Clayburn, Sharon O'Mara."

"Ms. O'Mara, so good of you to return my call so quickly. I heard you were in the area and I was wondering if you would like to have lunch with me this afternoon. There's a great little restaurant near the "The Tank." Could you meet me there at 1:00?" His voice was polished and sincere.

"The Tank?"

"Where the Sharks play, HP Pavilion. Small French place just to the west. Excellent food. Best, believe it or not, burgers in Silicon Valley."

"Now you're talking, yes. One o'clock sharp." She hung up.

The restaurant was faux French. The sign in gold leaf on the door said *Le Cage au Requin*. French lingo for The Shark Tank. The golden form of a shark sat directly below the name. Clayburn sat in the back booth.

"Cute place. Smells wonderful." There was an air and fragrance of Vietnam, Spain and France about the place.

"I tried to put all my favorite foods and places in here—makes it interesting every time you come in. But if there was one thing I wanted, it was a place people would drive miles just for a hamburger. Strange don't you think?"

"You own this?" She waved her hand about.

"Yes I do. When the Sharks came into town there was nothing in this area. A couple of friends and I saw an opportunity and we got in cheaply. We do very well during hockey season and after some pavilion events. We'd love to get another sports franchise in here during the hockey off-season. Would keep up the traffic." A short bull of a man walked up to the table wearing an impeccable suit, crisp red tie, American flag pin in the lapel.

"Hi Ross, good to see you, place looks great. Can you believe the win last night? The calamari was excellent—thanks for the support." He stuck his hand out toward Clayburn.

"Good to see you again, Mayor," Clayburn said with sincerity. "Five to two, great win, puts us just a few points out of first, right?"

"Yeah, just two." The mayor turned toward O'Mara, and flashed a smile that hinted at a leer.

"Mayor, please meet Sharon O'Mara. She's with an insurance company." Clayburn left the rest of the introduction hanging in the air.

"Glad to meet you, Sharon. One of our local companies or agencies?" he asked with a friendly manner.

"No, not really. I'm with Professional Life, investigating a murder." She smiled.

"Oh really. Well I wish you luck, good to meet you and good to see you again Ross. Let's get together for lunch sometime. I miss our chats." The mayor left quickly. The word murder was still hanging about the table like bad cheese when he reached the door.

"Mention murder and politicians run like the wind. You didn't need to mention that, did you? I've known Mayor Martinez for a number of years. He's a good politician and a good manager. Very helpful with this restaurant."

"And you support him financially?"

"I support a lot of good politicians in this area."

"Playing both ends against the middle, good way to insure your future. If the land stays in the county, you move forward. If the city decides to annex the land, you're ready to move into their General Plan."

"You're a very quick study, Ms. O'Mara. That's exactly the tact. With millions at stake, I must cover every base I can. San Jose will eventually take over the property sometime in the future. It may be cheaper to go through the county today, but eventually the approvals for individual parcels will be going through the city. It's good to have friends in as many places as possible." He waved to the waiter who had been patiently standing just out of earshot.

"Chen, a bottle of Pellegrino and ice please. I don't drink during the day, Ms. O'Mara. And if I can presume, two burgers with fries."

O'Mara smiled. "Burger rare, fries crisp, please."

"It didn't take very long for Pell to call you, did it Mr. Clayburn? He seemed a bit eager to assure me he's his own man. As much as any politician can expect to be."

"He's a good politician, but he has personal and financial problems. I'm trying to help him with some of these. But that's not why I asked you lunch. I want to offer you a job. I need someone who is tenacious and experienced, someone who understands human character and how to get things done. You passed the interview before I knew there was an opening."

O'Mara was taken back. She'd never been offered such a bald faced bribe—a flat out attempt to push her to one side of the equation, effectively neutralizing anything she did. And still, the offer was intriguing.

"Mr. Clayburn, thank you. I'm surprised and flattered. I obviously need some time to think about it. It's interesting in so many bizarre ways." Her cynicism wasn't wasted on Clayburn who understood from the beginning she'd never accept such an offer. He'd done it just for the reaction, and she knew it.

Lunch talk turned to sports and hobbies. When she pointed out the five hundred pound striped marlin over the walk-in fireplace, the conversation came alive. He'd caught it off the East Cape of Baja from a small panga almost twenty years ago. It was his first.

"The marlin was over half the length of the skiff, and fought it for two hours. Light tackle, only twenty-pound test; the young boat handler made the day for me. In fact, that young man now runs my Scarborough marlin boat out of Cabo—he's one of the best marlin captains on the west coast of Mexico."

O'Mara was impressed by how much this guy has done and how many things he has his fingers in. And someone who would go one-on-one with a quarter ton fish standing in a rowboat with tackle meant for salmon—remarkable.

Besides fishing, they shared car stories like a table of guys at lunch. When they parted they both had a bit more respect for each other. And the burger was the best she ever had.

7a

The planning commission hearing started promptly at
7:30 and lasted well into the night. The audience sat all to one
side, grouped around David Schenk. Like a wedding where the
groom's family doesn't show up, no one sat behind Cimoni and
Morgan.

O'Mara settled in the back of the hearing chamber in a neutral area. Rodriguez was giving a slow but detailed explanation
of the project. He described what changes had been made since
the last hearing and concluded with a summary of the anticipat-
ed scope of the Environmental Impact Report, the Specific Plan
and the forthcoming workshop with the Board of Supervisors.
The crowd on the bride's side continually whispered among
themselves during his presentation. The other side listened un-
responsively.

Following the planner's presentation, Cimoni went to the
lectern and thanked the commissioners and county staff for their
diligence and unbiased presentation. He walked toward one of
the large colored plans on the wall, noting the changes and significant adjustments to the plans. Turning to the audience, he
stuttered for a moment when he saw O'Mara. She couldn't help
but notice that he was almost pointing to the exact spot of the
shooting. Cimoni recovered and finished his presentation. Morgan, crisply dressed, stood and presented a thick black binder
of figures and projections to Rodriguez and the Commission,
apologizing for their lateness. She hoped they would be helpful
in understanding the projected tax revenues generated for the
County. There were no questions. She sat down.

It was the lull before the storm. The commissioners, almost in
unison, turned toward the left side of the room as the chairman

asked if there were any comments to be made by the public. Almost every hand shot-up. He announced that those who wished to speak must fill out a card. There was already a large stack on the table in front of him. He acknowledged David Schenk and asked him to proceed, noting that comments would be limited to five minutes due to the number of people who wished to speak. Schenk proceeded to the lectern.

"Thank you Mr. Chairman and Commissioners for the opportunity to speak out against this unfortunate example of poor planning. We have analyzed the concept in depth—its impact on prime wetlands, its unmitigated increase in traffic and air pollution, and its lack of schools, parks, and pedestrian greenways. This project is nothing more than the same old crap forced on us by developers for over 30 years. Where's the mass transit? Where are the buffers we need? And where's the traffic going to go?"

"This is leap-frog development." He was now in stride. "There are thousands of acres between this project and San Jose to the north. Why aren't those lands being developed? I'll tell you why: greed and the almighty dollar. These developers see land as only a commodity to be built on, then sold to the highest bidder. We lose wetlands full of endangered plants and animals, we lose our clean air, and then we have to sit for hours on the freeway congested by poorly planned growth. Why? Greed and one nastier bit I'm saddened to say, racism."

O'Mara's ears perked up when she heard the R word. So did Cimoni's. He turned and glared at Schenk, his dark eyes flashed in pure fury.

"Yes, racism. This community will be for successful white people. Yuppies, genxr's, and over-paid Silicon Valley executives. Where's the cultural mix? Where's the affordable housing? Where will the maids and gardeners live that service these people? Where? I'll tell you: miles and miles away—that's where. They'll have to drive to their jobs in this community since mass transit will be years away. They will add to the congestion and the pollution. We need better jobs closer to where these people live now." Schenk's audience erupted into cheers. Sharon could see not one of these concerned people would ever consider cleaning someone else's toilet, even for a hundred bucks. Schenk turned to the crowd and smiled. His gaze turned to Cimoni and Morgan as if to show them his strength.

"Commissioners, you have a duty to understand these facts. One, this development will lower the quality of life for everyone in the county. Two, the development will destroy countless numbers of endangered species. Three, this development will cause pollution that will shorten the lives of many less fortunate people who are not here to defend themselves. And fourth, but not the last, this development will put undeserved profits into the pockets of these people, money that should be used to provide housing for the homeless and less fortunate here in the county and in San Jose. It is your duty to protect the people and the environment. You must allow this development to move forward. Thank you for your time." Again the audience cheered their gladiator.

Schenk smiled to the commission. As he turned to take his seat, one of the commissioners asked, "Excuse me Mr. Schenk, I would like a point of clarification here. As you're aware, we're processing this development in a slightly different manner then normal due to its size and potential impacts. These impacts are being reviewed and analyzed in the EIR that's underway. That report is not due for at least four months. How is it you're so sure this community will have all those impacts you've just pointed out or are you guessing? We have heard this speech before and it may be good for the audience and the news media, but unless it can be confirmed during the EIR's assessment, they are just words. Empty words, nothing more. Where are your facts, sir? Because if that's what they are, then maybe we can cancel this process and save Clayburn Company hundreds of thousands of dollars in fees and costs? Where are your facts and where's their authority?"

Schenk smiled and collected himself, although his camp followers were collectively stunned.

"Madame, I wasn't necessarily stating specific facts regarding these elements of the community. My comments are stated as well informed opinions. Opinions based on my experience watching other developments like this. Almost without exception, any project over 2,000 acres will create all of these impacts. I stand behind what I've said."

Sharon's eyes followed Schenk as he strolled back to his seat. What an arrogant son of a bitch, but he definitely had bravado.

The chair asked Cimoni if he had any remarks. He stood.

"Mr. Chairman, if I presented our community plan to this commission with as much substantiation for our design as Mr. Schenk has with his comments, you would have justifiably shown my plan and me the door. We feel that all issues and impacts can be mitigated and made whole. Mr. Schenk's comments are incorrect and misleading. A veracity check would be in order."

Schenk jumped from his seat, "Are you calling me a liar, Mr. Cimoni?"

"No," answered Cimoni. "You are only someone who stretches his opinions into facts to suit his own purposes. You're not a liar Mr. Schenk. You're an opportunist and a provocateur. Nothing more—and nothing less.

Schenk began to push his way through the crowded row of collective knees.

"That's enough!" The chairman slammed down his gavel. "Both of you sit down. We have many more to hear from, and, if this continues one moment longer, I'll close this hearing."

Schenk and Cimoni stared full face at each other. In an older west, guns would have been drawn. Nowadays it's even worse—they both had loaded lawyers. The meeting had sunk O'Mara back into cynicism. They returned to their seats and for the next two hours listened politely to the public harangue about the evils this community would bring to the bucolic calm of the South County. If she hadn't seen the property for herself, she would have thought the site was a candidate for a national park. All it needed was trees so the spotted owl could return and water for the planned reintroduction of the snail darter. The strangest statement she heard was that, left alone, all the endangered species that never were on the property would begin to return. All they needed was a chance. Logic knew no home during these two hours.

After the chairman closed the hearing, he announced the plans for a joint workshop between the planning commission and the Board of Supervisors the following week. This workshop would be open to the public for their comments. He gaveled this hearing over.

7b

O'Mara strolled through the parking lot toward the rental, hoping she could remember what it looked like. Scanning the parking lot, she noted the lack of American-built cars. For a group gung-ho about local jobs, they certainly bought foreign. Volvos predominated. The old environmentalist standby, the Beetle, had become a BMW now. Her mood darkened as she flashed on Franklin and his BMW, where it led him and where it was leading her.

Standing next to the rental, she noticed a group of people a few rows over. In the dim orange glow from the overhead lights, she recognized Cimoni and Schenk. Loud words, a push from Cimoni, more words and suddenly two people grabbed Schenk and held him. Cimoni struggled against Morgan before being pulled away from the knot of people and dragged down the row of parked cars by his shirt front. Interesting. No—surreal.

She wandered over to Cimoni's car.

"What the hell are you doing here, O'Mara?" His eyes still flared from his encounter with Schenk.

"Homework." Her tone was matter of fact.

"Homework! What kind of homework would bring you all the way from Walnut Creek?" Doris Morgan's voice was acrid.

Why would Morgan know where I live?

"Oh, after the shooting of my car, my interest has no bounds.

And besides, there was nothing on TV tonight so I thought a good planning commission meeting would be entertaining. And, except for the two hours of droning by the audience, I was right. You should take your act on the road, Mr. Cimoni. You and Schenk make a good team. Good cop, bad cop, good and evil, Laurel and Hardy, take your pick. And the little bit of theater here didn't go unnoticed by either his supporters or the reporters." She hooked her thumb towards the white van with a satellite dish on the roof.

The two Clayburn employees turned toward the van, acting surprised when they saw the truck and two reporters standing next to it.

"Spare me. Your little act, even if one sided, was done for their benefit. I admire your bravado," she lied.

"All we're trying to do is build a new town for the future of California," recited Morgan. "A community for all people, no matter what that environmentalist ass says. We will have affordable housing, we'll build the schools, we'll provide twice the parks required and we'll have browns, white, blacks and yellows living together."

"That's enough, Doris. I think Ms. O'Mara knows all that and also understands where Schenk is coming from. You needn't go on." His manner was too abrupt, too abrupt to even an employee. Morgan's eyes flashed dark at him. No love lost here.

"Well thank you for the entertaining evening. I hope to see the two of you again at the workshop."

"You're coming to the workshop? Why?" Cimoni demanded.

"Like I said, there's nothing on TV as exciting as a planning commission workshop. I wouldn't miss it for the world." She turned and headed back to the car. Their eyes followed her the whole way before they each got into their own cars and left.

O'Mara stood by the side of her Japanese wonder car smoking a cigarette, watched them leave and then, after a stop at the Starbucks across the street, headed home.

7c

Three calls were waiting from Bryan. She punched up his home number and waited. Finally a gruff and grumbled answer, "This had better be good. It's one in the morning."

"Sorry, I didn't realize how late it was." Her voice was sweet as jasmine. "I was at the county planning commission hearing and lost tract of the time. I stopped for a bite at that Mexican restaurant in Pleasanton, now I'm talking to you with a burrito carnitas stuck somewhere in my gut giving me heartburn. A rough night lies ahead."

"Why do you do that to yourself? You know you can't eat this late and sleep and why the hell were you there anyway? If you've nothing to do, why don't you do it with me?"

"Kevin, please."

"OK, I'll drop it. Why there? Still can't shake this Franklin thing?"

"Yeah, that's part of it." She slurped the two-hour old frappaccino. "It's also that these characters are so full of themselves they're studies onto themselves. Anyway, I have a feeling there's something else going on that I can't shake. Doris Morgan, Cimoni's assistant, has no love for her boss. And Cimoni and Schenk almost got into a staged fistfight. It's a strange group of players. If it weren't for Franklin's death, I wouldn't give a flying fig for any of them."

"Flying fig, when did you clean up your language? Fig, oh my, oh dear."

"Oh shut up. Go back to sleep, I'll call you in the morning." She reached over and plunked the phone on the seat. Her eyes left the unlit freeway for a moment—just long enough for a dark pickup truck to swerve hard, directly in front of her.

She slammed on the brakes and the ABS system kicked in, cutting her speed by almost half. The truck also slowed, but not as much. Swearing loudly, and not referring to fruit this time, O'Mara cut hard to the right to get away from the truck. It matched her move. She cut back to the left and it moved almost in unison. She sped up to try to read the license. Its light was out and it sped forward at the same speed.

"No fucking games this time!" she yelled at the dark gate of the truck. She looked and saw the next exit was coming up fast. She pulled over one lane, it followed. She feigned a left. As it pulled left, she cut right, just catching the gore point of the exit. She took the short bump and sped up the ramp. The truck headed up the freeway. It never even hit its brake lights.

O'Mara pulled into an all-night gas station and waited among some parked cars for ten minutes to see if the truck backtracked. Nothing. She bought a hot coffee her gut didn't need, replaced the cold frappaccino with the coffee in the excellent cup holder the carmaker was proud of, and looked for her phone. It was wedged under the seat.

The rest of the trip home was—uneventful.

8a

Bars are probably the second oldest commercial establishments after village markets. In today's parlance they're "third places" like coffee shops, except for the welcomed lack of annoying children and the higher quality of the refreshments. Here all forms of entertainment and commerce take place: Sunday football; man's second most favorite pastime, drinking; and man's favorite hobby, in current lingo "hooking up." Sometimes out of loneliness, sometimes out of spite, and sometimes out of need, the parties get together, exchange niceties, negotiate terms, agree to an arrangement, and move the venue. The manager of all this social interaction is the bartender, and, next to priests and confessors, the really, really good ones deserve the seats in heaven Dante left vacant by the various rings and levels of hell he created for all those nasty folks. The best shakers and pourers have a stake in the bar or own it outright and, like the parish priest, create a home for the misunderstood, the lonesome, and the unappreciated. There are solid reasons for starting a joke: "A man walked into a bar . . ."

Gina Cavelli inherited Gino's after her father passed on to one of those great grandstand seats in heaven. She'd slid liquor up and down the mahogany bar for fifteen years on Mt. Diablo Boulevard. Still a knockout, a bit hardened around the eyes, Gina carried herself well and stole looks from most men walking down the street with her Loren-Lollobrigida look and movement. On the business side, she had over the years earned a lofty place in the social and cultural pecking order of the Lafayette business community with her charity, political support for the right people, and a good ear but even better managed mouth. She quietly made a lot of money in this rich town, but also added to it power. You don't serve drinks to locals for all those years and listen to their stories without developing a keen sense of local politics, business issues, and social comings and goings. More than money, it's information that has power.

Kevin Bryan sat at the end of the bar and shot up two fingers. Gina put a double Jameson on the rocks in front of him.

"Thanks, Gina, you look good tonight. Do something with your hair?"

Cavelli looked at him and laughed, "If I had a five for every time you said those words I would close this place and take you anywhere you wanted." Her hair—classically Italian-Greek, graying, no coloring, and as wild as the sea that washed the shore of her ancestral homeland of Genoa—sat piled on her head and held together with a large dark green clip. "So how are you, officer? Missed you the last few weeks. Anything new about that BART thing?"

"That's why I'm here, to avoid discussing any of that stuff. I've had it up to here and need a chance to just think and talk to one of my favorite women."

"There are others?"

"Hundreds—they just don't know it yet." Bryan took a long sip and let loose a long, soft sigh.

"Like burping a baby," Cavelli offered with a smile. "Better?"

"Getting there."

A call from a table caught Cavelli's attention and she moved out from behind the bar to take an order. Bryan's eyes followed but were snagged by a short brunette sitting alone at a small table wedged in the corner. She saw his look, smiled and saluted him with a pink-drink-thing in a glass. What the hell—he took his drink and filled the empty chair across from her.

"Kevin Bryan. Come here often?"

"Ouch, that's awful. Can you do better?"

"Maybe, we'll see. You're new here—I know most everybody."

"Business meeting in Walnut Creek, had to get away from

the boys, if you get my drift. After five days of meetings, I've heard all the jokes and stories, and if I see one more picture of wifey and the kids, I'll sock someone. Needed to get out of town to avoid them and this looked like a good bar and it's just a short walk from the BART station—no car and staying at the Marriott. It seems to have worked out. And now, with you here—I assume no wife and kid pictures—good liquor and music, I can finally relax. I'm Denise Moran, accountant, big Chicago outfit, here to train plebes as we say, Mr. Kevin Bryan."

"No wifey pictures, and the music is good." Bryan shot a quick look at Gina. "Two more, Ms. Cavelli, if you please."

Gina's smile flowed into a brief but knowing what-the-hell-are-you-doing look. Bryan passed on it and continued his conversation with the overly attentive Ms. Moran who had accidentally loosened her white blouse to expose at bit more cleavage while mentioning the heat in the bar. Bryan smiled, got the drinks at the bar, and rejoined his best new female friend.

"There, better?"

"Much. You seem to know a few people here. You've a local business or something?"

"I work for the city, a civil servant if you please. Just my hourly and overtime is all I've got. It's enough, and the benefits are not too bad—plus somewhat regular hours. So here I'm, able to spend some time with a pretty young lady from Chicago."

"The line is getting better, Mr. Bryan."

He raised his glass. Small lie. Young is not a word he'd use again. Layers of makeup helped to plaster-over the furrows and canyons around her eyes. *But what the hell, got nothing better to do.*

The conversation drifted around business, California weather, and other banalities. She'd be here for a week then back to Chicago before another week on the road in Cincinnati and Pittsburgh—all training and all very boring. Now? …. live on the north side near Wrigley, no boyfriend, too busy, never home long enough, hate the travel but love the percs. Did you know I have over a million miles on my American Airline card? Going to Europe for a month, maybe next year." For his part he acted very interested—maybe he'd get lucky.

"Well I've an eight o'clock tomorrow, a presentation on the new federal accounting requirements. I'd rather sleep in." She pulled a small paper from her purse, took a studied look and said, "There's an 11:12 I can catch and be back to my room before midnight. Nice meeting you Kevin, maybe next time." She stood to leave.

"If it's not too forward, may I drive you to your hotel, only a little out of the way? You'll be home way before twelve and still get a good seven hours."

She looked down, smiled, and put the paper back in her purse, "Well, sure, why not. You look like a decent guy, and the bartender knows you—always a good sign."

She looked over to Gina—who was watching Bryan with a you-better-not-do-that-young-man expression—and smiled like a cat with a mouse under its mitt.

Three whiskeys relaxed Bryan to the point of being loose and carefree, the most relaxed he'd been in weeks. He waved to Gina as he left the bar in the narrow wake left by Denise Moran. Gina didn't wave, but gave him another disapproving look and mouthed, "Be careful."

Careful, he thought, I'll be careful as he watched the tight blue-jeaned butt of Moran bounce down the sidewalk three paces ahead of him. "Denise, the other way, just up the street, this way."

"Oops, sorry." She turned, looking a little unsteady on her heels. "Lead on, sir."

The drive took five minutes, the negotiation in the front seat, two more. The heavy kissing and groping another three. The invite, ten seconds. The elevator kissing and stroking a full minute. The key fumble, ten seconds. The offer of a mixed drink and the mixing itself, one minute. The niceties of pre-sex negotiation, barely two minutes. More kissing and clothing removal, a bit over fifteen seconds. The head swimming and eyes glazing, precisely twenty seconds. The falling down and passing out, instantaneous.

8b

Bryan woke with the worst headache he could ever remember, sans clothes, wallet, shoes, watch, underwear and self-respect. He found a nice fluffy robe to cover his embarrassed ass. *Well this is a new one—me a cop and taken for the proverbial ride. God she was good, and when I find her I'm going to have her ass.*

He sat on the end of the bed and thought it through. *Shit, I am a sorry son of a bitch,* came to mind first; second, need to get out of here; and third, how?

"Sharon, I know it's early."

"Early? It's ten o'clock. Why do you think it's early?"

He looked at the clock again: 7:05 on the digital read out. "One second." He clicked on the TV to the weather channel, in the lower corner it read 10:05, and changed to 10:06 as he watched. "Crap . . . I need your help. Do I still have those jeans, tennis shoes, and sweat shirt at your place?"

"Yes, I keep them in a place of honor, why?"

"Bring them over to the Marriott room 420. I need them."

"Marriott, 420, Mr. Bryan what the hell have you gotten yourself into?"

"I'll tell you when you when you get here, soon I hope."

Twenty minutes later Sharon O'Mara politely knocked on the door of room 420, a bag of clothes under her arm and a long list of questions on her mind.

Bryan took the clothes, "No underwear, sorry." She smiled.

"I guess commando," he called from the bathroom.

Bryan laid out the embarrassing evening—she insisted on details—and how he ended up here. At least he'd left his gun at home. He'd already called the station to report his ID stolen. He'd make a full report later in the day. Didn't explain to the chief over the phone—he'd meet him in an hour.

"You really are a sorry SOB Kevin Bryan, and at Gina's! Please! You know as well as I do, you never hunt in your own back yard, and this is exactly the reason why."

At the desk, Bryan asked a few question. But without his ID, they were reticent about divulging any information, especially since a tourist abduction incident from a room in San Francisco a week ago. Yes, he understood, but "could you give me the name of the person who rented the room?"

"A Mr. William Bonney," the clerk said.

"William Bonney, you sure?"

"Yes, it's right here, paid with cash."

"Okay, Bonney. A guy, a guy? Description?"

"Yes, five feet four inches, wiry, hard."

"Cash, no credit? Listen I'll be back with my badge with some more questions. By the way is there an accountant conference for a big financial outfit here this week?"

"No, only a three-day Jehovah Witness executive meeting," the clerk answered.

"Do you know who William Bonney is?" O'Mara was unusually cheerful this morning.

"Yes I do. Billy-the-fucking-Kid. Shit—I am a sorry son of a bitch."

Also taken was his car. O'Mara gave him a ride home, where he changed into proper and more comfortable clothes—Bryan never realized how itchy-scratchy no underwear could be—then to the police station, a BOLO on his car, and a three-page report listing his stupidity and missing ID. Sharon nursed a Starbucks down the street while Bryan finished the paperwork. The chief, while sympathetic, still insisted on a two day unpaid leave while they sorted everything out.

While he waited for O'Mara to return, a report came in from the Walnut Creek police that his car had been found, parked on the street two blocks from the BART station within two blocks of the Marriott.

"Glad she decided not to drive home. Said she was going to take BART home and I guess she finally did."

9a

Leaving early for the late morning joint meeting of the planning commission and the Board of Supervisors workshop didn't help. It only allowed Sharon to sit for an additional hour waiting for traffic to move. Nobody likes to live near where they work. It's a contemporary American tradition. The result of this personal indulgence is traffic that begets more traffic that equals accidents in a macabre post-modern ratio of mess equals distance divided by traffic lanes. Passing the tangle of colored metal, melted plastic, and flashing lights, she realized that one car was a tortured match to the one she was driving. She studied the road more intensely the rest of the drive.

The Clayburn project was again presented to the assembled group, Rodriguez then Cimoni. Then the commissioners and board asked questions. This meeting was more informal—open shirts, comfortable cotton dresses and western boots. Herman Pell was modeled on the original Hollywood cowboy—checked shirt, jeans and alligator Luccheses, a stark contrast to Cimoni's dark double-breasted pinstripe suit, Morgan's elegant knit and Schenk's heavy cottons and work boots. O'Mara was sure if Cimoni owned anything casual, it probably had a horse and rider on the breast pocket. He always wore his cotton over silk, reverse of her silk over cotton.

Pell questioned Cimoni in detail about the development of the community, its phases and expected impacts—both pro and con. He asked about environmental issues, wetlands, plant and animal species, open space areas, and most importantly, traffic. The community was centered in his district and he wanted to understand it all. O'Mara was impressed by the questions and scope of the answers. Following Pell, each of the Supervisors asked their questions, many rehashing Pell's. Had they been listening?

After an hour and a half, the chairman announced a short break followed by questions from the audience. He stressed the point of questions, would not tolerate rants, lectures, or unproductive speeches. A grumble rose from the crowd, gaveled down from the dais.

"I see you made it, Ms. O'Mara," Doris Morgan politely offered a sardonic smile. "Do you find these workshops interesting?"

"It's my first. And as with most first times it can be exhilarating, strange, or just plain scary. In this case strange stands out. Everyone is going through the motions as if this has been rehearsed over and over. All the life's been sucked out of the discussion."

"Just excellent preparation, Ms. O'Mara. We've spent a lot of time educating the board and the commission about the community."

"And a lot of money, as well. The slippery political slope to hell is paved with dollars, as they say."

"Be very careful, Ms. O'Mara. This is a very important project to a lot of people for many reasons, reasons that you're not aware of. So I offer you this bit of womanly advice, walk away from this now." Morgan turned on her sharp heels and joined Cimoni who was being quietly berated by an older woman dressed as if she had drifted in from an Amish kibbutz. He smiled during the tirade, but Sharon could see his eyes kept flashing toward her. They were not smiling. A gavel clacked hard against the podium and the workshop was called back to order.

"We have time for only a few members of the audience to speak. This workshop will be over at 12:30 due to other meetings this board must attend. There will be many opportunities for questions at later meetings." A grumble like distant thunder ran through the assembly. "So let's begin. The first speaker is David Schenk with Green Ridges. The audience turned toward Schenk. He was damp with sweat; his forehead glistened and to

O'Mara's eye, looked uncharacteristically nervous, far too nervous for his experience. He set his hands on the podium and looked toward the board and commission members.

"Thank you for this opportunity to present Green Ridge's comments." His knuckles were white. "As you're well aware, we have been against this development from its first presentation. Our primary reason was the plan's inability to deal with environmental issues in a forthright manner. Today, though, we have seen how, by proper planning, many of these issues can be planned for and properly addressed."

O'Mara wondered where he could be heading.

"Since our last public meeting, we have reviewed the plans again, and we have listened intently to the presentation this morning. We feel confident the plan has moved dramatically forward. It is our belief that if this spirit of cooperation were to continue, this development could be made acceptable to Green Ridges. Thank you."

In stunned silence people stared at Schenk in disbelief over what their ears had heard. What had just happened?

O'Mara's eyes found Cimoni. He neither raised his head nor acknowledged what had been said. He only continued to write in his notebook.

"Next speaker," announced Supervisor Pell. For the next forty-five minutes, speaker after speaker addressed the board. There was no cohesion, little common thread between them. Each group presented their complaint and sat down. It was obvious the head had been snapped off. But how, and more importantly, why? There were few questions from the board, some requests for clarification, but little substantive discussion. The public portion of the workshop was closed.

"Ladies and Gentlemen of the Board and Commission," Pell concluded, "I believe we have come to a consensus, even though we have many months of review before us. Most of the public's concerns will be addressed in the environmental impact report. The few new issues are minor and will be easily included by Mr. Rodriguez in the final report." Pell looked at Rodriguez and nodded. "Therefore, I move that this Board go on record as supporting the general concept and goals of this community plan. The Planning Commission can do as they please."

The motion was immediately seconded and although some minor discussion continued among the Supervisors, Pell and his arguments overshadowed two of the board members and their opposition to the plans and the continuation of the workshop process. The motion passed the board three to two, the dissenters noting they only wanted more time. The planning commissioners refused to take a vote.

The audience never stopped whispering during the discussion on the motion. They were louder during the vote, a roar when it was done. Pell had to call for order just to get the floor to close the workshop. It had definitely ended with a bang not a whimper. The board filed out and the spectators began to rise and leave. No one looked at Schenk. He picked up his oversized briefcase and walked to the rear of the hearing room where an older woman in a long cotton dress and short pageboy stopped him. The room was silenced by her full hand slap across Schenk's face. "You goddamn traitor, fuck you!" She spun on her Birkenstocks and led the rest of the audience from the room.

Sharon gathered up her notebook and saw Cimoni standing in the front of the room. Morgan was collecting papers and plans. Cimoni, smiled at the slap and Schenk's non-reaction.

"What the hell just happened?" O'Mara asked no one near her. She turned away from Cimoni and followed the others out.

9b

Leanne mechanically drove up her hips to meet his thrusts. She had done this a thousand times and she would do it a thousand more. It made her a good living that left her in control. She manipulated her hips to provide the hardest contact with the least pain and pushed faster. This guy at least could ride it out. Most came in two minutes when she was like this. Schenk had staying power.

"Hold it a second, I'll role over."

"No, this is great, I love to watch you."

She knew her breasts were her best features, the best bill-boards she had. It was hard to decently show off the rest. Her mind wandered, as it always did, while she lay there. *Get into the city to pick up a silk blouse at Bloomingdales, have dinner with some old politician a new client wanted her to tease, and see if the money had been deposited.* It was always there on the 10th, two thousand dollars. All she had to do was lay this Schenk guy when he wanted it. He was easy to schedule, always in the afternoon, same place, two hours, and the rest of the day free. Sometimes he wanted it twice a week, sometimes every other week. Every time he complained his schedule wouldn't let him see her more often. Big deal. With her butt and tits she could pull in an extra five or six thousand a month with this guy's regularity. Business was very good.

It's a shame this idiot hasn't a clue what's going on. She smiled.

Schenk's breathing and penetrations quickened. She liked this part, watching their faces congest and contort, squinty eyes rolling back, sometimes they almost blacked out. A few watched her watching them. She was at her best, her head twisting back and forth to match her hips. Sometimes she stuck her nails into their ass to get them to push harder. Men, when they were like this, were a piece of cake to push any way she wanted. She felt his hips begin to shudder and then the familiar pressure. She still pushed and squeezed; she didn't want it said her work was incomplete job. She liked the excitement of a rubberless job. That's also why she insisted on professional businessmen—better chance of being clean. Though she still used medications—just in case.

Schenk lay still for a few minutes, breathing hard and deep, then rolled over on his side. He traced circles around the small dark nipple on her left breast, then pinched. She let out a sensuous ouch and laid back against the pillow, stretching her arms and legs into a long and lanky oriental softness that hid her wiry strength. She could do things with her body he would never discover.

The coconut scent of her hair reminded him of those three weeks in Belize and that environmental meeting on the rain forests in Central America. All he remembered was the great shit they smoked and coconut smell of that University of Colorado piece of ass he screwed the whole time. She was twenty years younger; sure that what she was doing was helping the movement. The only movements Schenk remembered were those she made with her no tan-line body.

Schenk swung his legs over the bed and strutted into the bathroom. He was in good shape for a middle-aged socialist, the mirror told him. God she felt good. He ran his fingers through his grayless black beard. Her smell hung about his face. Later when he sat in another of those council meetings, like the one he had tonight, all he had to do was rub his beard and the afternoon would come back.

"Leanne, I need to get going. I need to get back to San Jose and the traffic will be the shits. The workshop this morning left everything up in the air, have to control the damage and sooth some egos. Couple of problems to correct."

She knew that already. The call explained enough and the few extra bucks didn't hurt. She casually called Schenk at his office to set up this visit—although he thought it was his idea. She looked into the mirrors on the wall and, like him, admired what she saw. She pulled a white silk chemise over her head. It hung on her nipples for a moment before softly sliding to her waist. She slid her legs into leather slacks, stretched them up toward her hips. They felt cool against her bare legs. The chemise covered the strap at the waistband. A leather jerkin then covered the chemise—it was a tough looking outfit. He loved it. He sauntered out of the bathroom, gave her an admiring glance and put on his own clothes—denim shirt, corduroys, work boots, and tie. His shirt had a whale where someone else would have a polo player.

"God, you look like shit, man. If my friends saw you they would laugh me out of town."

"Pretty strange, isn't it? It's a uniform, comfortable, cheap to keep clean, doesn't threaten little old ladies. Occasionally even convinces the powers that be that I'm more honest than the suits. And it doesn't seem to hurt donations either."

She smiled and languidly turned away from him. He took another long look and still couldn't figure her out. He'd always had a thing for Orientals. They were a lot different than the New York shiksa he was married to. Leanne never asked for money, never said no, and thank God, never wanted to discuss politics after screwing. She always smelled wonderful and dressed like a million dollar model. Sure, she probably screwed other guys, but he didn't care as long as she screwed him. And best of all, she loved the way he screwed her.

9c

They slipped out the motel door into the damp Oakland air. The roar of traffic on MacArthur Boulevard drowned out their conversation. A heavy mist had settled in. They had both parked down the street. The motel insisted he prepay, in cash, before the bald guy with the Grateful Dead tattoo gave him the key. The headlights up Broadway were a continuous dotted white line one way, red the other. They waited at the corner and watched the timer on the crosswalk march down from ten to three. They started to cross. The black Mercedes sitting at the curb, like the space shuttle in the final moments of a NASA countdown, roared its huge engine, and, with a squeal of its tires, covered the fifty yards from where it had sat idling. Timing the stop light perfectly, it lunged through the turning traffic directly at Schenk and Leanne.

The chrome bumper slammed into Schenk mid-thigh, nearly snapping him in two. His upper body bent unnaturally onto the top of the hood and flew over the corner of the sedan. His legs cart-wheeled after the torso and he met the curb with his head. His neck bent awkwardly. Schenk's body cushioned the bumper's impact on Leanne Wu for a nanosecond before the unrelenting mass drove her down into the street and rolled over her. Her leather gear, like a biker's, prevented the rough abrasion of the street grinding across her skin, but it couldn't absorb the five thousand pounds rolling over her hips twice, front tires and then back. Not a sound from the couple as they lay in the street. Cars piled up at the intersection, doors flung open, drivers jumped out. The huge sedan's tires squealed until they regained the asphalt, turned right at the next corner, and disappeared into the night. Two dark shapes were left in the intersection surrounded by onlookers—some concerned, some curious. Wu's small purse disappeared from where it fell two feet from her body. Someone asked Schenk how he was doing. When there was no answer, liberated his wallet.

Schenk would be very late for his next meeting.

9d

The conductor's baton plunged downward precisely at 8:00. Puccini's luscious *Turandot* filled every carved detail of the San Francisco Opera House. Allen Cimoni was alone, as usual, dressed in an elegant tuxedo. He always dressed for the opera, unlike a growing number of people. It pissed him off to see sports shirts, and even denim, in the audience. He was the last of the elegant breed: educated, refined, and rich. Many had two out of three, but few had all three.

He was satisfied with the turn of events since Schenk's capitulation. What a whiny pushover he'd turned out to be. One call to his home, housekeeper answers, would David call him back. Schenk's return call lasted all of five minutes. Schenk said little, Cimoni said a lot. The results were obvious from the workshop. Allen Cimoni was sure their plans would sail through. True, all the usual costly bureaucratic baloney still needed to be attended to, but everything else was fine—excellent, in fact.

The drive back to San Francisco that evening from the workshop was remarkably easy—a good sign. He'd changed his clothes in his office and taken a cab to the Opera House. Parking was always a hassle and he could be certain his car would be safe in the Clayburn Tower parking garage.

There are cars, there are automobiles, and then there's the Mercedes 300SEL, 6.5. In 1973, the luxurious black sedan had no peer—none could touch its power, appointments, wood trim and chrome, glorious chrome on almost every edge, corner and frame. Cimoni never tested its maximum speed, but he knew it could fly if he tickled the pedal to the floor. The sedan was an extension of him, an elegant reminder of who and what he was. Its restoration was complex, very detailed, and well done. The odometer read 220,000, but it looked as if it had just rolled down the gangplank from Germany. He'd spent a full day studying the details on a sister ship in the Mercedes museum in Stuttgart. The museum itself had intrigued him, so he hired the same architects to design an office building for Clayburn.

Always punctual, he arrived early, saw no one worthy of greeting, and sat in the private Clayburn box, an indulgence Ross Clayburn allowed himself, though he himself seldom attended. Cimoni knew the tenor parts by heart, hummed them to himself. The irony of the opera wasn't lost to him. Turandot was brutal and treacherous, full of riddles and fatal answers to the wrong questions, with a woman who used politics to get her way. A style Cimoni admired.

After the intermission, Cimoni stayed behind in the lobby to finish his champagne; the second act began slowly, no reason to rush. He decided a quick walk around the Opera House would leave him alert for the second act. Setting his empty flute on the window ledge of the grand entry fore court, he walked down the steps and turned toward Franklin Street. Dampness hung in the air from a brief evening shower. His Saville Row tuxedo held the cold back well.

The line of red traffic lights up Franklin Street to the crest at Geary Street mixed with the red taillights. Cimoni blinked and the lights all flashed green at the same time. Maybe the champagne dulled his senses just a bit, maybe it was the cute blond at the bar—whatever the reason, Cimoni wasn't on guard until he heard and felt his nose crack and break against the cold stone surface of the building. Maybe it was the rough black cloth bag being pulled across his face, squeezing pain from his crushed nose. Maybe it was when his tuxedo jacket was pulled down from his shoulders to trap his arms against his sides, or maybe it was when a fist went deep into his stomach and pushed nausea up into his throat. Whatever it was, he quickly regained his senses and lashed out. Letting out a primal scream, Cimoni pulled his arms upward, ripping the stitching up the side panels of his tux, spewing buttons across the sidewalk. Quickly freeing his arms and continuing to yell with a fury that chilled the already cold night; he spun and kicked out toward to where he thought the assailant was. His knee hit bone, his shoe caught soft tissue, and a guttural noise and a sharp clink of steel on concrete came in response to his brutal reaction. Freeing one arm, he pulled the bag off his head while continuing to punch and kick the collapsing figure. He flashed on the thought the bag was actually a woolen cap—that explained the stench. He finally saw his attacker—thin to almost gaunt, blood pouring from his nose, a pained look in his sunken eyes. Cimoni kicked hard at the side of his knee. The thug screamed and collapsed completely to the sidewalk.

The security guards rounded the corner of the building in full gallop. A giant of a black man slid across the damp sidewalk and caught himself before he collided with Cimoni. "What the hell's going on in here?" he hollered. Cimoni stopped kicking and backed away from the figure sprawled on the sidewalk. The second guard pulled his nightstick and cautiously walked toward Cimoni.

"This son of a bitch tried to mug me," he said, to the guard with the stick, blood dripped from his nose to his lips. "Just trying to take a short walk around the block before the next act and this son of a bitch jumped me. Pulled that stinking stocking cap over my head and started to rip-off my wallet. The sorry prick quickly found out no one messes with me." The black guard looked down at the prone figure and saw the glint of a knife just before the blade sliced through the air toward Cimoni's leg. The guard brought the shaft of his nightstick down on the flailing arm. The crack of bone was followed by a howl. Both guards hit him again. They pulled his arms behind him hard, and cuffed him.

Cimoni stood back. Served the son of a bitch right. One of the guards bent his head into the microphone pinned to his shoulder. Within thirty seconds two San Francisco policemen pulled up in squad car, lights flashing. The assailant was moaning in pain, ignored for the moment.

"Goddamn, I just need some money," the bum mumbled into his shirt. "It should have been easy-easy—just pop him once, get his wallet, get out of here. How'd I know he's some goddamn Rambo type?"

Cimoni turned quickly toward the mugger, "What did you say?"

"Fuck you!" The cop pulled his arm tighter. His scream filled the street. "Fuck you, you asshole." He withered as more pressure was applied. The cops tried to stand him up, but he collapsed back to the sidewalk.

Ten minutes later one of the guards helped Cimoni through the lobby and down to the men's room. Seeing himself in the mirror shocked him: bloody shirt, torn tux, split lip, nose already swelling.

"Wonderful, just what I need, a broken nose. This ends what was a pretty great day. At least the fucking bastard got what he deserved."

With the bleeding under control, Cimoni answered the sergeant's questions for another twenty minutes and then caught a cab home.

10a

When Cimoni woke the following morning, everything hurt, or so it seemed. Sitting at the kitchen counter, he drained the third cup of coffee the maid had made and delicately massaged his right hand. Of all his bruised body parts, it hurt the most. The coffee's warmth ran up his fingers, softened the ache in his knuckles. The four ibuprofen seemed to have finally started to cut the pain. He unfolded the Chronicle. Splashed across the header in bold letters topping the right hand column, "Environmentalist Killed." Scanning down he read David Schenk had been the victim of a hit and run in Oakland. The popular activist had been killed and another pedestrian, an unidentified woman, was severely injured. The driver and the car hadn't been found.

"What the hell?" he said out loud.

The telephone rang.

"May I speak with Mr. Allen Cimoni?"

"Yes, this is Allen Cimoni."

"Detective Sanchez here, Oakland Police Department. Do you have a few minutes?"

"Yes, what can I do for you?" he answered, still trying to read the article about Schenk. His tone was a bit impatient with the officer.

"Did you hear about Mr. David Schenk?"

"Yes, I'm reading it in the paper right now." His radar went up. Attorney Allen Cimoni wasn't going to volunteer any direct information, he was sure of that.

"We're calling those who might have had contact with Mr. Schenk during the last few days, especially people who may have attended the hearing yesterday. I understand you were there?"

"Yes, I was. It was a workshop, not a hearing—big difference. We have a project before the board and the workshop took a good portion of the morning."

"Could you tell me where you were after the workshop?"

"Drove back to San Francisco and changed my clothes at my office for the opera."

"And later in the evening?"

"I was going one-on-one with a thug outside the Opera House. He tried to mug me. I've got a bruised face, busted nose and one very painful hand. That jerk didn't look too good either when they hauled him off. Talk to Sergeant Wang with the SF police, he'll fill you in."

"What kind of car do you drive?"

"A 1973 Mercedes sedan."

"Color?"

"Black."

"You returned to your office after the meeting? Which side of the bay did you use?"

"101, why would I go through Oakland?"

"You tell me," Lopez demanded.

All the questions revolved around his actions and where he was the night before, three rounds to be exact, all asking the same questions but differently. Cimoni had enough.

"As you know I'm a lawyer. I've been giving you straight and honest answers; any more questions from this point forward will be directed through my own attorney. What the hell is this all about? I was in San Francisco from about three o'clock on. According to this newspaper article, Schenk's accident happened about six o'clock. Why are you calling me? If I'm a suspect, then file charges. If not, please leave me alone. Besides, there were hundreds of people at that hearing. I hope you know Schenk's unexpected support of my project angered many of them. Are you questioning all of them?"

"Yes sir, we've started questioning some of them. You were close to the top of the list. I'll check with Sergeant Wang. We're looking at the rest, at least those we can identify. And Mr. Cimoni, it wasn't an accident. We'll call you later. Thank you for your time."

The detective had riled him up. Who the hell did they think they were, and what did he mean: "it wasn't an accident?" Cimoni had just found out about it from the paper—how'd he get to be a suspect in a hit and run. *Well screw'em.*

Cimoni called his office to say he was staying home. He answered Morgan's questions about the mugging and his health. He smiled when she called him a hero. He also had to get things together for his dinner party tonight. Oh, there would be stories to tell and wounds to show.

10b

O'Mara placed the articles she'd clipped from the morning newspaper in front of Bryan, along with a manila envelope. He was on the phone. He said good-bye and turned to face her, annoyed.

"Do you know anything more about all this crap?" she asked.

ENVIRONMENTALIST KILLED IN HIT AND RUN, read the first.

DEVELOPER STOPS MUGGER AT OPERA. This one in the society section.

He didn't open the envelope, but scanning the clippings:

Special to the Chronicle: David Schenk, 40, was killed in a hit and run accident in Oakland last night. Another person, Leanne Wu, was severely injured. Schenk and Wu were struck as they crossed MacArthur Blvd. at Broadway.

Schenk, activist/president of Green Ridges Intelligent Protection Electorate (GRIPE), was a well-respected environmentalist and supporter of open space and ridge lands protection. He employed a style called confrontationalist in his public meetings, a style he learned with Greenpeace in the early eighties. Schenk's family has been well known in civil rights

and labor actions since the McCarthy era. His parents, both attorneys, challenged the blacklisting of local writers, defending them against being labeled communists.

Schenk was currently leading opposition against a new community proposed for southern Santa Clara County.

Witnesses describe the hit and run vehicle as a large black sedan, possibly foreign. No arrest has been made. Schenk is survived by his wife and mother.

Leanne Wu was crossing the street at the same time as Schenk and was also struck by the same car. The police are investigating the accident as a hit and run and are withholding additional information until specific leads can be followed up.

Mugger Gets Mugged

Bon vivant and now, it seems, crime fighter, Allen Cimoni, senior legal beagle with the Clayburn Company (see Clayburn Tower) duked it out with a mugger on the streets in front of the Opera House last night. The fisticuffs took place during Puccini's Turandot, which seemed wholly appropriate. The thug was placed under arrest and taken to the hospital by police. Witnesses say the assailant was definitely the loser of the fight. He was bloody enough to warrant an ambulance, rather than the patrol car. "Rocky" Cimoni could not be reached for comments.

Kevin looked up.

"As a matter of fact I do know something more about this crap. Oakland police say the car was traveling at least thirty miles an hour, didn't brake when it hit Schenk and Wu. A witness said it was an older black Mercedes or similar luxury car. One fellow, who was a little drunk, said the car had been parked for over a half an hour in front of a nearby motel."

"What motel?"

"The motel the paper didn't mention in the story. Schenk and Wu were seen leaving the motel just before they were hit. The manager said they had taken a room there about three hours earlier. They used the room "often" was his comment. Oakland says it was very messy. Schenk was killed instantly, shattered skull. Wu broke both legs, an arm and her pelvis. She probably won't work again."

"Did she work for Schenk?"

"In a manner of speaking—by the hour, a very classy hooker. Took a few hours to find out who they were because a few good citizens confiscated their IDs—and cash, I suppose. She had a few arrests a couple of years back, but nothing recent. She owned a Lexus—at least it's in her name. It was parked up the street from the accident. Why Schenk was with her, other than the obvious, Oakland's not sure. They're still talking to motel manager. Oakland has not had a chance to interview her yet—hasn't regained consciousness from her surgery. No head or facial damage. She's lucky. Was Schenk the guy you were telling me about? The guy who changed his stance against that Clayburn property?"

"Yes, he's the one. Vehemently opposed it in front of the Planning Commission, then at the Board workshop yesterday he felt sure there was common ground they could stand on. It left the door open for further discussions. The open door allowed the Supervisors to push for a vote. Looks like someone murdered him."

"Looks like it."

"I visited him at his office, tried to understand where he was coming from. Now he's dead. It's weird. I'm sure he was set up. Who would know he was at that motel unless they'd followed him or was informed he was going to be there. If his involvement with the girl was a set up, the driver knew about it and tried to kill them both. She was lucky, kind of. There's a big chunk missing. Why all this over land and money?"

"It's fairly common, I'm afraid."

"Yeah, I know, but the money in this deal will take years to materialize. Too long a time, too much can happen. There's a sense of immediacy here, violent immediacy. Someone wants something now, not five years from now. I wonder if that's what

Franklin was doing with those papers. I keep going back to who knew I would be out at the property and when. Clayburn and Cimoni were the only ones other than you. Clayburn gave me the map, right? Cimoni left a bad taste in my mouth trying to be smooth. You know, at the Planning Commission and Board hearings he was very thorough and professional, never lost his composure. Even smiled when Schenk equated him with the worst society can create—bringer of disease, famine, and pestilence sort of stuff. Cimoni just sat there, shook his head and took notes."

"At the Board workshop Cimoni presented the general outline of the Plan and Morgan gave the specifics and the design concepts. They pointed out where modifications would be made and why. They completely addressed Schenk's and the Commission's comments in the presentation—sort of an olive branch to Schenk. Schenk, for his part, was lukewarm, not at all vitriolic. Quite a change from my meeting with him before the hearing."

"Who's this Morgan?" Kevin noticed the unopened envelope.

"Assistant to Clayburn. Sharp, late thirties early forties. Pretty good looking but with a touch of muscle. Must work-out a lot. From her answers to the Board, it's clear she knows development—works directly with Cimoni."

"The Board was asked for a consensus vote based on the revised concept. Pell was the swing vote, three to two, to continue the plan along the direction proposed. Cimoni saw it as a victory. Pell insisted on the vote." O'Mara wiggled her butt to get comfortable in the city-issue metal chair in front of Bryan's desk.

"Seems normal."

"It is. I talked it over with one of the county planners, fellow named Rodriguez. I met him few weeks ago before all these meetings. He said these votes always happen. To give the proponent faith in the system. And it allows him to keep his bankers happy. Really doesn't mean a thing until the final votes on the EIR and Specific Plan, which are months away. The vote really spooked the staffer Rodriguez, though."

"You said Schenk changed his stand against the development?"

"Yes, or in fact just modified it. Surprised almost everyone, infuriated his followers—everyone except Cimoni. He didn't even look up during Schenk's presentation, just took notes. Pell jumped on it though. The crack allowed him to set and drive a wedge. The vote was that wedge."

Bryan's telephone rang. "Yeah. Thanks." He hung up.

"We can't talk to Miss Leanne Wu. She threw a clot from the internal damage and had a stroke. She died on the table. Four dead people now and the only common thread is Clayburn. What's in the envelope?"

"Something you don't want to see."

"Why?" He opened the flap.

"I found these at my house, in the mail slot. Your little tryst has me involved now."

Bryan slid the papers out of the envelope: photos of him in awkward and embarrassing poses. A short typed note was clipped to the top.

Dear Ms. O'Mara,
Drop your involvement with this Clayburn investigation or these will be delivered to Officer Bryan's chief.

It was unsigned.

"I don't like where this is going," Sharon said. "I'm unlisted and no home phone to connect to an address. Only a few people would be interested in setting you up to get to me. What the hell's happening?"

11a

Sharon called a few days later to set up a meeting with David Schenk's wife and her attorney. This, she thought, ought to be as comfortable as sitting in the waiting room of the dentist while there's a root canal without gas going on in the next room; all you can do is wait your turn. She climbed the stone steps of the three story Berkeley Victorian.

"Good morning. May I tell Mrs. Schenk who's calling?" A tall, severe woman wearing a soft dark gray cotton dress, hair pulled back in a bun, wire frame glasses on her sharp nose, and eyes the color of winter stood at the open door looking down directly into O'Mara's eyes. The woman's gray eyes were bloodshot from tears.

"Yes. I'm Sharon O'Mara, an investigator from Professional Life. I called earlier to arrange a short conversation with Mrs. Schenk about a case I'm working on."

"Yes, Mrs. Schenk said you would be by, please come in." O'Mara followed the wraith down a dark wood paneled hallway that opened into a sunlit room. It took a few moments for her eyes to adjust to the glare. Sitting on a floral divan was a woman at least seventy, quite a contrast to the woman at the door. Dressed in a soft shade of yellow with exceptional makeup, she sat as the centerpiece in a room with flowers on shelves and tables.

"Ms. O'Hara, I am Ruth Schenk. How can I help you?" The question was direct and almost without emotion.

"I assume you're David's mother and not his wife."

"What a stupid and rude comment. Of course I'm David's mother. Judith, David's wife, is returning from England and will be here late tonight. It took us two days to locate her. She's tremendously shattered, just as I am. You're the tenth person to stop by today to see if everything is all right, and as you can see, it's as good as it can be—all things considered." The bitterness was palpable. "Who are you Ms. O'Hara insurance person, and why are you here?"

"O'Mara, Mrs. Schenk. I called earlier to meet Mrs. David Schenk to get a better understanding of what happened to David. Obviously I was led to believe by someone here that his wife was in. I've wasted my time, I can see that now."

"Yes rude and impertinent too; the police and now you. What the hell can I tell you that I didn't tell them? Judith is at an international conference on women's issues and the environment. She's been there for almost two weeks. When I finally was able to talk to her about David's death, she fell apart and I had to get the hotel to assist her in making the arrangements to fly home. No, we don't know who this Luann Lu person was. I've never heard of her. And lastly, I was shocked to find out what she was and what she was doing with my son. She obviously trapped him into this arrangement and some jealous client of hers killed them both." Ruth Schenk was at least to the point. Unfortunately for her, O'Mara didn't buy it.

O'Mara's eyes swept across the room and looked out the window, she stood and walked to the glass wall. The garden was just beginning to green up, a few azaleas were blooming. She looked back at Schenk and wondered why yellow was preferred over black, at least the housekeeper wore gray.

"Her name was Leanne Wu," Sharon Said. "The police may have believed all that, but I don't." Her back faced Ruth Schenk. "I've seen her type before—only one of many, right?" She turned. "He couldn't help but exercise his manly rights on anyone who would fall for his line. You've been around the political scene long enough to know that power and sex go together. But in the case of Leanne, I think David was the one being used. He was so caught up in his own ego, he couldn't see it. It was a fatal mistake for both of them." She was getting tired of the games being played.

"How dare you. What right do you have coming into my home and chastising me? Don't you know who I am?" Ruth Schenk stood; she was almost six feet tall.

"Oh I've a good idea, but unfortunately I came here to meet the wife of David Schenk and her attorney, not the woman who made him what he was."

"And what's that?" Ms. Schenk stared down at O'Mara with a glare that would freeze stones. "I raised him to be the perfect social activist, to right the wrongs that have been done to the poor and disenfranchised. To help in every way he could to change the direction of this country from its headlong collapse into . . . "

"Capitalism." Sharon finished her sentence.

"If you will. Yes, into that social abyss of capitalism where only the rich are rewarded and everyone else is left to serve these self-appointed masters. I raised him to think beyond that, to realize we're a social whole that must fight to preserve our freedom from these tyrants. It's only then we can help all the people. Only when we have taken back what they've taken from us can we be truly free."

"And of course its agenda is what you and your group determine it to be, since you're the leaders, right?"

Ruth Schenk returned to the couch and stiffly lowered herself. "I'm sorry but I've been on edge recently and the death of my son has made it worse."

O'Mara couldn't believe what she was hearing—not the words, but the demeanor. Schenk was grieving not like a mother but more like the teacher who had lost her best student. This is one cold son of a bitch. O'Mara could easily understand why David Schenk had a callous disregard for morals and for women. He had learned well. She guessed Judith Schenk was an approved marriage of socialist equals and would be no different.

"Mrs. Schenk, I came over to ask a question that's a part of an investigation involving a shooting death. Do you know anyone named Richard Franklin?"

Schenk stared at her for a moment. "No, I don't believe so, but I meet so many people. Is he a politician or something?"

"No, he's a dead bookkeeper. Thank you for your time." O'Mara turned to leave. The gray wraith appeared from nowhere.

"Stop by anytime, I would love to continue our conversation." Ruth Schenk nodded graciously as O'Mara left the room.

"Yeah, right. I'll be right back—not a chance."

When they reached the door, the gray woman opened it and in the same motion passed a square of paper into Sharon's hand. And just as quickly she was outside with the closed door hard behind her. She squeezed the paper tightly.

She drove a few blocks with the paper still in her hand. She pulled over to the side of the narrow street and slowly unfolded the paper. On it, in neat legible handwriting, was a short paragraph.

Ms. O'Mara,
They all knew about David and his personal activities. They tolerated them because they needed him more than he needed them. And they knew it. It scared them and they were afraid he would leave them behind. His cause was greater than theirs and they knew it. They are dinosaurs and David was leading a just cause to save the planet. I'll miss him.

"Great. Another one of David's conquests—living in the same house! What a nest of snakes." She re-entered the flow of Berkeley traffic. "Only one more day and I'll have my baby back. But I'll miss these cup holders."

11b

The drive across the Bay Bridge to San Francisco was a disaster. The University Avenue on-ramp was blocked with construction, so O'Mara took San Pablo to Ashby. It was only marginally better. The wait at the tollbooth was stop and crawl. Once on the bridge it was nose to butt. Traffic will kill us all, she thought, as she eased her way down into the city.

Clayburn agreed to meet her at his offices at 5:00. He asked whether she had dinner plans. She said that she had. She could kick herself for not accepting considering his dinner plans were probably significantly tastier than hers, but she was getting tired of everyone's games.

She parked on the first level of the garage and took the two-elevator hop to the granite and mahogany foyer of Clayburn's office. Doris Morgan was nowhere about. The receptionist spoke softly into her headpiece, then quietly stood with an elegant air and preceded O'Mara down the hallway to Clayburn's office.

The setting sun washed the room with a shimmering of oranges and yellows, specks of dust danced diamond-like in the shafts of light. Clayburn stood looking out at the city's radiance. "Are you here to accept my offer of employment?" he asked with a wry smile as he turned. "I could really use someone like you."

"No, I don't think so Mr. Clayburn; too many people die who are involved with you directly or indirectly. It is far too dangerous a job." As if on cue, the sun slid behind a building on Russian Hill and the room darkened.

He was dressed with an elegance that bespoke real money and earned ease. Soft cashmere pullover and dark gray slacks that were far cry from the grays of Berkeley.

"Why are you here then? You turned me down for dinner and you now insult me. I'm hurt beyond belief." He clasped his hands together over his breast in mock pain.

"No pain intended, but the rest is true. Do you know anything about Leanne Wu?"

"Who?"

"Wu."

"Wu who?"

"Stop that!" He was a charmer. "She was the hooker killed with Schenk yesterday. I'm sure you've heard all about it by now. Was she in your employ? Stands to reason since Schenk usually went for girls who he could as you might say—impress. And a thousand dollar a night hooker was way out of his style and price range."

"She wasn't working for me. It's not something I go in for. I like the more direct way—helping out friends who may need a boost in their campaigns, some help with expenses. Hookers and drugs are something I seriously abhor. Ever since my time in the Far East I've found those activities—repulsive and, more often than not, counterproductive. Money is easy to explain and manage. Drugs are dangerous and can bring in the police. Besides they can render the subject stupid, if not dead. I like smart, wide-awake politicians. Folks who focus on their next piece of ass are not much help either. They're scared to death to be caught, but just can't give it up. I do believe though, that Schenk was into that type of weakness."

"How do you know that?"

"I had him followed a few months back and this oriental chick was a bi-weekly deal. I've no idea where he got the money for such a luxury. The pictures of the two of them were kind of funny. She was a knockout in her usual leather. He looked like a Berkeley professor. If anyone saw them they would think he was dating one of his students—so many Orientals at Berkeley." Clayburn walked to the bar. "A drink? It is after five."

"Please, Red Label, rocks."

"Coming up."

The sun was returning from behind a building. Color returned to the room. The lighting slowly rose and faded as the sun disappeared and returned. She took the scotch from Clayburn, careful to avoid his hand.

O'Mara kept the edge on the conversation. "Strange last few days, the surrender of Schenk and his death; Cimoni in a fight."

"That was a hoot! That punk at the opera didn't know what he was getting into. Cimoni was a boxer in the Marines. The mugee mugs the mugger. Kind of poetic justice, Cimoni has a shiner and a busted nose, but not as bad as what happened to the other guy." Clayburn smiled. "That will teach them to try to rob people at the opera."

O'Mara smiled, noticing how Clayburn didn't offer any more information on Schenk.

"What's going to happen to your San Jose project?"

"Which one?"

"The south San Jose new town. With Schenk dead, what will happen now?"

"No impact. Schenk is a non-issue and with his death the environmental groups will fall apart for a while. It may be a year or two before someone emerges to whom they might listen. Assumption to power in those groups is messy and noisy. I like elections—they are much more predictable and democratic."

She noted his assessment was probably right on target. Like street gangs the environmental movement's leaders all fight their way to the top. There's no such thing as egalitarian elections in the environmental movement. "The whole mess is convenient, isn't it?"

"What do you mean?"

He's unflappable, this guy!

"All your troubles have vanished in the last few hours. Pretty convenient."

"Yes, I guess so, but I still don't have the final approval. That has to come through the supervisors. This publicity will delay the project a while longer. In this game, time is money—a hell of a lot of it."

O'Mara walked to the window. Clayburn's eyes followed her. The sun, standing low between two buildings at the crest of Nob Hill, created a halo around her head. Her shadow fell directly on Clayburn.

"I still don't get it. Why are you holding on to this whole Franklin thing? Let it go. The man's been dead over a month and they've a suspect in jail. Let it go."

"I can't. This is so personal now that even my company is trying to get me out of the case. They've closed the books on their part and are insisting I do the same. It's just tough though, after being shot at, to give up. I need to know what went on. I need someone to pay for the damage to my car."

Clayburn was taken aback by her last remark. "Your car?"

"Yes, my car. Nobody shoots my car and puts me out a couple of grand and gets away with it." She put the empty glass down.

"I'll pay for your car. In fact, if you come to work for me, I'll get you a new one."

"Nice offer. Bribery will get you everywhere, but then again you know that. No, I won't work for you, Ross. Thanks for the drink. Got to get in line to cross over the bridge."

"The dinner offer stills stands—traffic will be gone when it's over."

"I think you mean in the morning and that's not even on the table."

"I seem to be a bit embarrassed. I meant nothing of the sort."

She started toward the elevator, stopped, turned, "By the way, how long has Doris Morgan worked for you?"

Clayburn seemed taken back. "Let me think. Five years, maybe seven. Yes, seven. Met her in Hong Kong. She helped on a project I was building. Liked her work, offered her a job here. Smart girl, tough as nails, why do you ask?"

"Nothing, just wondering. She around tonight?"

"No, she's not. Had some follow up to do on this Schenk thing, she said. Needed to look at the future strategy, since he's out of the way."

"I'm sure she does."

The bridge was a nightmare.

12a

Sharon's cell phone rang, dragging her from a dreamless sleep. Something she hadn't had for a month. Unknown number glowed on the screen.

"Hello, this had better be good." Her smoky voice had an ungracious edge.

"Ms. O'Mara?"

"Yes, this is O'Mara. Who the hell is this at this ungodly hour?"

"Doris Morgan, from Ross Clayburn's office. We met a few weeks ago at Clayburn's office and I've seen you at the hearings."

"Yes, fine and well, my office is open when the sun is up. Not in the middle of the goddamned night." She paused hoping Morgan would hang up. There was a long silence.

"Obviously this is not a social call. What do you want?"

"We need to talk. I know some things that you want to know. And an exchange of information might be mutually advantageous."

"Sure, what do you know?"

"Can't talk, my phone may be monitored by Clayburn's security. Ever since those papers were found, he's been a demon about security."

"What about now? You've already used my name, your name, and his. If privacy's such a big deal they'd certainly know by now, wouldn't they?"

Another long silence followed. "I'm on my cell, should be a bit safer. You're right, I screwed up, but we still have to meet. How about tomorrow, for lunch, in Lafayette? I'll be at the new apartment building site for an inspection all morning. There's a coffee shop on the square. Do you know it? Meet me there at one o'clock. Okay?" Morgan's voice had a nervous tinge.

"Fine, see you then." She lay in the dark, thinking. The red glow from the clock silently changed from 3:05 to 3:06. *What does this mouse want to tell me? Or maybe she's a rat.* She rolled over and fell back to sleep.

Basil's nose was one inch from her face when her eyes opened. His puss stretched across her limited horizon. He took one big sniff and sat down to watch her get up. If she didn't know better, she'd swear he was a voyeur. A voyeur dog with an I've-got-a-secret grin. Yes, in some, if not most respects, he was better than a boyfriend.

She took a quick shower, dried and combed out her red hair. She felt comfortable in the reddish brown pull over and jeans. Peanut butter toast and dark French roast had her awake by seven o'clock. It was only then she remembered the telephone call. Perhaps it was a dream, but she remembered the clock changing so was sure it happened. Lunch in Lafayette at one. Gave her time for a couple of hours at the range before meeting Morgan. Six or seven clips might loosen this tension and paranoia. She bought Basil off with some milk bones and headed out into the garage.

The Jaguar looked good as new, only $1,200 to cover the damage. $1,200 she didn't have. Reginald was a dear, but that blew her trip to Cabo San Lucas. "Somebody is going to pay for this—with interest!" Mexico was her one great release and joy.

The range was not crowded and she scored well, consistently. The Beretta 92F was a precision tool—similar to the pistol she carried in Iraq. Unlike Iraq, here it was something she could control and it gave her security. She left relaxed with it safely cached in her bag.

She checked in with Bryan. He had nothing new to report, but no liquor showed up in either Schenk or Wu. No drugs either. "Rocky" Cimoni was silent, or at least was giving no interviews, except to the police.

"And about your little adventure?" she asked.

A long pause. "Be a good friend—please just leave it alone. My badge was found in the car along with my wallet. Only the money was gone—along with what little pride I had left. The pictures were printed on a cheap printer, no possible follow up"

"Serves you right and mom says don't ever do that again—and you know I'll cover your back."

12b

Morgan was waiting for her in the last booth against the wall, no window behind her. She stood as O'Mara approached, extended her hand and smiled. "Thanks for coming. I wasn't sure you'd remember my call."

"I remembered. What do you want?"

"To the point, good." The waitress put a cup down and Sharon nodded. The coffee cup was filled to the brim.

"I've some information you may want regarding the death of David Schenk."

"Yeah?" Her interest rose considerably, though she refused to show it.

"I believe he was setup by Cimoni. That girl who died really didn't work for Schenk. She was a call girl or something. Cimoni introduced her to Schenk at a fundraiser a few months back. Why Schenk was there, I'm not sure. It was a fundraiser was for Herman Pell and he and Schenk usually didn't get along. Anyway, she was a pretty Chinese girl in a tight blue dress. Schenk talked to her most of the night. They left about the same time. I recognized her from the photo in the paper. Schenk's people said she was an associate. They were probably embarrassed by his actions and were trying to protect his wife and family. Get the press to believe he was a pure right thinking fighter for morality and good."

"And Cimoni?" O'Mara asked and wondered why all this information.

"He drives a black Mercedes 300SEL sedan. He loves that car. Very rare."

O'Mara swallowed a little coffee—nothing she'd come back for. "Interesting, sure. Why bring it to me and not the police? They are the ones who could use this information. You know you're withholding valuable information—they could arrest you." It was a threatening bluff, and she got the reaction she was looking for.

"Do you think so? Oh, no. I thought that maybe you could take it to the police. That way Mr. Clayburn doesn't know the information came from me. If Cimoni gets in trouble for what I said, Mr. Clayburn wouldn't forgive me. I need my job. It's all I have."

"That's okay. You should at least let the police know. They can be quiet when it comes to these things, especially a murder investigation."

"I will, I will," Morgan responded, with almost too much enthusiasm.

"If what you're saying is true, Cimoni had something on Schenk. Blackmail maybe, or at least some other type of leverage. I wonder if that's why he modified his support for the development."

"That's my guess. Remember, Schenk became very conciliatory with Cimoni about the project—talked about options, alternatives and flexibility. It was a far different point of view than when he was in front of the Planning Commission. There he was adamant and unbending. In fact, Schenk almost took a swing at Cimoni in the parking lot after that hearing. Schenk's people pulled him away before they could go to blows. Cimoni was still calling him out as they drove Schenk away. Cimoni can be very nasty when it suits his purpose, but I'll bet he'd always make sure the other guy took the first swing."

"You know I saw that," O'Mara said. "Nice act."

"Schenk had a crowd of his followers with him and I think he was trying to impress them. Cimoni smiled and called him a lying son of a bitch who needed an audience to perform to. That was all, but Cimoni's tone infuriated him."

"But between those two meetings, something happened,"

Morgan continued. "Cimoni was unbearable in the office during the week between the planning commission meeting and the workshop, like he was holding a trump card. Maybe he was. Then at the workshop Schenk toned down his invective so much I thought he might even endorse the project."

"So what's the why, Miss Morgan? That's what I want to know."

"My guess is Cimoni let it slip that he knew all about the little oriental prostitute and he would let the right people know if Schenk didn't change his position. Obviously something happened. Now they're both dead. Personally, I think Cimoni hit them and left them to die."

"You don't much like Cimoni, do you?"

"No, I don't, but I do like my job and I work for Clayburn. Ross is a straight forward guy. I've been with him for seven years, two years longer than Cimoni. Cimoni is younger, I've more experience. I'm a women, he's a man. 'Nough said."

Oh great, O'Mara thought, an equal righter, just what I need. O'Mara knew there was an imbalance, but she got to where she was by being better, like most men have to. Between working hard and being better, better works. Not whining about it, but being forceful about it, in their face if you have to.

Morgan stood up and drained the last sip of her orange juice. "I've stayed too long, Ms. O'Mara. I hope what I've given you was helpful." Morgan set her handbag on the table. The muted sound of metal on Formica sound caught her ear—the same sound her Beretta made when she put her bag on the kitchen counter. *Very interesting.*

"Yes, you have. Please do call the police."

"I will, I will." Morgan said. O'Mara doubted it.

She watched Morgan cross the street and get into her car. A Ford something, a sensible car. She picked up Morgan's orange juice glass with a napkin and poured out the last drops of the juice into the half empty coffee cup. She slipped the glass into her bag, left a five on the table, and followed Morgan's trail out the door.

12c

"How about dinner tonight?" Sharon asked Kevin. "I need to drop off something for your lab boys to check. I'll treat. Can I get your okay on the fingerprint test?"

"Yes, I'll let Don know. And no way! Dinner at my place: spaghetti, bread, and a great cabernet. Meet me at the office and follow me over."

"See you at six."

Sharon put the cell phone on the newly oiled bucket seat next to her. Morgan had an angle working here, but you also could see the acting. This was one broad who didn't sit back and take it. She gave as good as she got and she was sure Morgan was priming her for something—but it wasn't yet clear what.

She grabbed the cell and punched in Clayburn's number.

"Ross Clayburn, please . . . When is he expected? . . . Two o'clock? Can he meet with Sharon O'Mara at 2:30?" She waited out a thirty-second pause. "Great. I'll see him there."

She turned the Jaguar toward the Bay Bridge and San Francisco. Even the traffic agreed with her trip. No delays and the downtown jumble was almost bearable.

She parked in the Clayburn building. The top floor lobby had changed since her last visit. A large model sat to one side—the condominium project in Lafayette. It was going to be grand. Pool complex, parking, entries, plazas, new retail facing Lafayette's main street and four floors of housing.

Clayburn's reflection appeared on the glass, producing a strange overlay—like the structure and he were synonymous.

"Impressive isn't it? These will be the first new condos in that town in ten years. Yet they still made me beg to build it for them. Times are very crazy. So much housing is needed, but it's only us bad guys who can provide it. At the hearings, they make me out to be some devil who will steal their very souls if I enter their little town. And by the way it is a pleasure to see you two days in a row. A real pleasure."

She turned. *God he was a package.* She could go for someone like him. She winced and internally slapped herself.

"Did I say something inappropriate?"

"No, no. It's just that—so, why do you do it if it's such a royal pain in the ass?"

"In fact, I've retired twice. It's not the money or the fame—not even the power those two can exert. Believe it or not, it's because I like to build things—and now I have resources to build big things, things that make an impact. Like that property in south San Jose. The money's secondary."

She laughed.

"No, it is true! I'm worth millions and can have anything a boy could want. But it's the satisfaction of beating them to create something for the future. My legacy is in the projects and buildings that will last a few hundred years. My money will disappear down some government rat hole, that's for sure. But the buildings will stand; the roads will provide the community fabric into an unseeable future. Did you know there's a road outside of Rome that has stones first laid over twenty five hundred years ago—and it's still used? That's my dream and legacy."

Sharon walked over to the expanse of windows; "A week of sun and the goddess of winter gets jealous." The room was gray; fog through the Golden Gate obliterated the sun; buildings further up Nob Hill were obscured by the damp haze.

"I meant that job offer. I don't meet someone with your tenacity very often or with your investigative talents. You'd be a great asset to my firm. I know you refused and I understand. But let me be specific: travel, a new car, and far more money than you're making now."

"Thanks again Mr. Clayburn, but I like the freedom I have. Sure, I'd like to give Basil a T-bone every night, but all things considered, it could be worse." She still couldn't shake the earlier image of him from her mind. His earnest proposal was sounding better with every moment.

She needed to break the spell. "What do you know about Doris Morgan?"

"Why do you ask—for a second time?"

"Just professional curiosity. She's at all the hearings and seems to have a good sense about her." She hoped to draw him out.

"Well, I like to keep her to the back of the firm. I give her jobs that require research and data collection. She keeps the consultants in line and calendars for the various projects."

"Does she make important decisions regarding the projects?"

"No. All decisions are mine. The tough ones are made after Allen and I review our options, but I make the final call. Why the interest in Doris?"

"It's tough to manage people and their egos, isn't it? Sometimes it's hard to even know what may be going on directly under your nose, if trust is too highly placed."

"What do mean by that? Or should I ask what do you know about my company that I don't?"

"I'm not sure yet. But Morgan came out to see me this afternoon and tried to peddle some stuff about Cimoni and Schenk. Even said she thought it was Cimoni who hit Schenk and the hooker."

"Really," Clayburn answered, shocked.

"Surprised? Probably was setting me up to make sure I told you what she said. Loyal employee and all very concerned about the firm and what Cimoni might have done."

"Allen couldn't have done that."

"You're absolutely right. He was in San Francisco beating up a bum at the opera house.

"Just what I need! Bullshit at all levels—inside and outside this business. I'll ask Doris about it when she gets in. If it's what you say—and I'll be able to tell—she's gone. I need a full team, no one pulling against the flow. Thanks for the information. But why would you help? Me and this company don't mean jack to you."

"Let's say I've a professional responsibility to my former client, the deceased Mr. Richard Franklin. If helping you helps me find the killer, so much the better."

"Drink?"

"No thanks—got to get back across the bridge, date tonight."

"Lucky guy, and who is this Basil fellow I am jealous of?

"My dog."

13a

Dinner was comfortable and full of past memories. Sharon was concerned Kevin would begin to fall apart after the second bottle of wine. He kept looking at her with that lost look he got after scotch and cabernet. She'd known him on and off for over ten years. He had just joined the Lafayette police after a ten-year stint in Oakland. He needed some rest he said — rest after all the chaos in Oakland. She was also a rookie — and after six years in the Army MP's, half of it in Iraq, she'd found a nice break in the claims department of Professional Life. They'd met again over a murder-suicide with two young kids left sitting in the living room, a big chunk of money, and total confusion. Bryan wasn't shocked by what he saw — just where it was. She'd seen this kind of carnage before — but only in war. Peace was hard to find, even in the suburbs.

She worked closely with Bryan to get the kids to child protective services and eventually to relatives well outside of town. The oldest sent her a letter a few months back. He seemed well adjusted — junior in high school — starting what looked to be a successful life. But the hardballs he would still have to deal with would come high and tight.

She dropped the orange juice glass off at the same time she picked up Kevin. She told a white lie — it was about another case — but suspected that he didn't buy it. He'd probably check the results before he gave them to her, but not too deeply. He signed the paperwork.

His place was a small cottage in the hills overlooking Highway 24, a testimony to the solid architecture of the 1920s. O'Mara wondered how one guy living alone could create such a disaster.

Women can be messy, but guys leave a profound neglect that stirs the soul. Clothes were not the issue; there were a few ragged piles. It was the magazines, dirty dishes, and disorder that shocked her. It was good he didn't have any pets—they might not survive.

He also had the biggest heart of anyone she knew. How entangled he was with so many lives after his years on the force, she hadn't a clue. She knew of kids whose lives were straighter due to him, their grades sent to him to confirm their progress, a few whose lives had been saved by his efforts. The meat grinder of the underbelly of Oakland forced him out and through the Caldecott Tunnel to Lafayette. He saw death in Lafayette so seldom; he was shocked when he arrived at the Franklin scene. It still stuck in his mind—loop after loop, dark edges, slashing rain, wet crimson in the bull's-eye from his flashlight, blue and yellow strobe lights—they came back in the staccato flashes of an old movie.

For all the good in the man, a bad marriage and even worse divorce left him sour and financially screwed. Luckily, there were no kids. His wife left him because he spent more time with his collection of survivors than with her. Even O'Mara was included in the blast zone. There were subtle suggestions during the divorce their friendship was more than professional. Some days during the legal hell, all she wanted to do was give him a warm shoulder, but she knew that would only add to his confusion. For all his problems, she loved the guy—like a brother. The brother she never had.

"Saw Clayburn on the tube last night—man that guy is photogenic. Looked like an English lord or something. Quite a character."

"Missed it." She hadn't let him know she'd been with Clayburn not three hours ago. "What was he doing?"

"Something to do with the new Giants' ballpark and a luxury apartment complex he's going to build next door to it. Walk from your luxury apartment to your luxury box without even stepping outside was his comment. Those guys don't miss a chance, do they? Anyway, there're going to be two hundred luxury high-rise units, and the mayor and a couple of the supervisors joined him. They made an interesting group. My guess they haven't been to a ballgame in years, if ever—let alone bought a ticket with their own dime."

"Cynic! Of course they've been to games, just look at how they supported the new park and helped move it along."

"Who's being the cynic now? Anyway, Clayburn's man Cimoni was also there looking dapper with his black eye and wrapped hand, quite a celebrity after his scuffle with that bum. A couple of questions were asked about his escapade. He was sorry he had to miss the last act of the opera, poor baby. That guy gives me the creeps. Some stand out from the crowd so much that you wonder why they are not politicians or in jail."

"Cynic back on you." She filled his glass again, dark red flashing in her mind. She shook her head. *What's going on? Ross has his fingers in so many things. Damn it, get out of my head. Go, out. Now.*

Bryan leaned back in his chair, hands behind his head and looked at the ceiling. "Sharon, where do you think this thing is going? Nothing points to one person, yet the dead and injured keep piling up. Sure a lot of it points to Clayburn, but it could easily be someone else. Maybe there's more than one out there shooting and running over people."

"That's possible. To kill someone, unless you're psychotic, is usually intended to silence them—keep them from saying something or pointing back to you. It changes how the murderer acts—one less thing to worry about, one less problem. If all these dead people were problems, why were they a problem? And to whom?"

"The most obvious is Cimoni, the second is Clayburn, and the third until a few days ago was Schenk. Two left."

"Two left that we know about. I keep coming back to Franklin. It's pretty clear he was an innocent, unlucky schmuck. But, what was in his briefcase that got that boy shot?"

"Two thugs, if I remember. And one was maybe a murderer.

Oh, I forgot to tell you, the state lab got back to us on the brief-case. No other fingerprints, but dried blood in the seams of the briefcase matched the DNA of the dead kid. It's obvious the case was in the car when the kid was shot."

"If it was money, they'd have taken everything." O'Mara said. "The only thing clean was the case itself. No fingerprints except for Franklin's on the inside? Strange. Why not just dump it where it would never be found? Haste? Lack of opportunity? Or just the need to get rid of it? Maybe all three."

"Too many directions, too many victims. I'm going to bed, coming?" he asked again for the one-hundredth time.

"Please. Not tonight, I have a headache," she answered for the hundred and first. "I'll call you in the morning."

After a light kiss on cheek—barely more than a handshake—he walked down the hall. Sharon took her coat from the back of the chair and headed toward the door. "Good night, Mr. Bryan." Something muffled followed her out.

13b

O'Mara pulled into a parking stall on Mt. Diablo Boulevard, dragged herself into Gino's, chose a stool at the end of the bar, and smiled as the bartender walked over to her.

"How yah doing kiddo? The usual? You look a bit rough on the edges," Cavelli said while wiping down the bar. "You need to see me more often, I miss your smiling face." O'Mara and Cavelli went back a few years—before Iraq, the Green Zone, and Bryan. O'Mara always left a few bits of intelligence about the neighborhood and Gina reciprocated. She slid the tumbler between Sharon's hands.

"There, Johnnie will make you feel better. Guaranteed."

"Thanks. Do you remember that killing in the BART lot a month or so back? I'm sort of involved—dealing with a claim on one of the people shot. Still trying to piece together the story. Can't find the killer."

"Same case Kevin Bryan's working on? Franklin was his

name, right?"

"Kevin? How do you know that?"

"He stopped by here a few weeks back, said he was glad to get a chance to relax."

"Oh, so this is where it started!" O'Mara's eyes twinkled. "That memory of yours still amazes me. Why do remember that?"

"Started what? Started what with Kevin? Wasn't that wiry bitchy thing, was it?"

"Oh, nothing—just a little trouble, but he worked it out. Someday he'll tattle on himself."

"Franklin came in here for a while, you know, maybe two, three years ago. He was a regular for about six months. Perfect gentleman, had a Stoli up, usually only one. Talked with me a bit and with Jack, you remember Jack—he was here for about a year before the Marriott opened and he went there. More diverse clientele, you know."

O'Mara nodded and smiled. Jack was a hunk until she found out she wasn't his type or anyone of her sex's type. Big disappointment.

"Nothing remarkable, but Franklin struck me as someone who had his life together, 'cept for a dark cloud looming somewhere close. So what did happen to Kevin? It was that small assed brunette, wasn't it? Told him to be careful."

"Did he ever talk about his business deals? Franklin—not Kevin." She feinted, protecting Bryan.

"Not that I remember. Seldom talked about his personal life, but in a humorous, old-fashioned way called his wife his 'ball and chain.' It was that chick, wasn't it? Did she give him a ride or something?"

"I've met her, the wife. He wasn't joking. And yes it was, and yes she did, and I'm not saying anything more. He'll have to tell you the story—his way."

"Fine, Franklin never brought her in. You know, for many a bar is a refuge from family. For others, it's a cave to hide in. I listen, and when I can, I help their poor souls. But you know, for some there's no hope, their souls are lost. Doesn't happen much, but when it does, it can be one hell-of-a serious disaster. Franklin was fine, don't even remember his first name, didn't seem to have problems he wanted to discuss, never bitched. He had that rare thing—a good attitude. I've seen all types over the years, and he struck me as a good guy. Liked him, but he moved on. Haven't seen him for probably two years now. His killing was a kick in the gut, I'll tell you. Excuse me." Gina turned to other end of the bar. "I'm coming. I'm coming. The usual, Charlie?"

Gina ran her damp cloth down the length of the bar as she left. Sharon sipped her scotch.

Gina ambled back a few minutes later. "If I have to make another Mojito in my life, it'll be too soon. Those damn Bond movies set serious drinking back twenty years. Shaken, not stirred." She wiggled her butt. "Stirred, shaken, who the hell cares. Then that top heavy broad comes climbing out of the sea like a buxom goddess, asking for this frou-frou drink. Some days I've so much mint back here I think I'm at the f'en farmer's market. Can you believe I had someone ask if the mint was organic? In a bar mind you, organic? OK, where were we? Yes, Franklin and Bryan." Gina took a gulp of air.

"Did he ever say anything about Clayburn Company?"

"You mean those guys building that condominium complex across the street? Not that I remember. Are they involved? A couple of the workers and a foreman come in here a couple times a week after work for a beer. Never seen any of the white shirts though."

"No, not really." She hated to lie, but information is a two way street—you're never sure where it goes after it leaves you. "Just a note about that condo was found in Franklin's pocket, but it seems to amount to nothing."

"Good, we need those condos here—rents and houses have gotten ridiculous for this sort of neighborhood. Maybe a few more units will ease the demand and put a few more butts on my stools."

O'Mara and Cavelli chatted a while longer—men, dogs,

men, Bryan. "Nothing I can say now, nothing …" Sharon kept saying. She left a nice tip and then strolled out to her almost better than new car.

13c

A soft sheen covered the Jaguar and its newly painted skin. The flashing lights from the pizza joint across Mt. Diablo Boulevard reflected in the dew and wax. O'Mara ran her finger along the side of the car, a spray of water followed leaving a thin line from bonnet to boot. She rubbed the moisture in the palms of her hands, smelled the earthiness of late evening and the slight touch of acetone from the new paint. The car felt cool and fresh. *Funny how we attach ourselves to things: cars, pets, and men. Shit, I need to get a real life.*

She drove under the BART tracks that split the town in two, past the hundreds and hundreds of homemade crosses on the slope that faced the station platform, each for a dead American in Iraq. She knew a few of those names. The crosses always took her back there, but not in the way the people who stuck them in the ground wanted. She only remembered their bravery, their honor, and for some their death. She parked in the BART lot. It sloped uphill from the station toward the freeway whose noise masked sound so well you couldn't hear the person standing next to you. The pavement, soaked from an early evening shower, mirrored the freeway and overhead lights, adding visual cacophony. Strings of moving headlights flashed from right to left and left to right. Orange flares from the overhead streetlights radiated across the lot producing a dramatically different scene than when she walked the lot in daylight after the shooting. The edges were now indistinct, the noise louder, more muddled. Whoever fired the shots had to be very good, even if they were close—anything over a hundred feet would have required an expert marksman. She lit a cigarette.

She played the scenario over again on the almost empty set. A Subaru wagon sat near where Franklin's BMW had been. The path to where the two kids ended up was clear. The noise from the freeway and the rain meant the carjackers had to scream at Franklin to be heard. Adrenaline would have been pumping, adding to the confusion. Maybe Franklin put up a fight, maybe he shoved the kid. The guy who shot the kid—and the one who took the briefcase—would have been tracking Franklin, not the kids. Franklin had what he wanted. The kids only complicated how he'd get it.

Reviewing: this guy is following Franklin trying to get to the briefcase, maybe kill him if he has to—but these two dudes suddenly appear, two predators competing for the same prey. The briefcase guy holds back long enough to see the carjacking begin, realizes his booty is going to be stolen and fires at the kid with the big chrome pistol. But misses because of the rain, kills Franklin instead. The kids freak, jump into the car. Maybe the tire is flat, maybe from the kid's chrome cannon. They take off, lose control, and crash. Briefcase guy walks over, pops the driver and sees that the other is out. He looks for the case on the floor of the front seat, sees it in the back and drags it over the dead kid smearing his blood on it. He splits. But how? And to where? O'Mara scanned the lot, past the highway, past the platform, past the crosses, to the brightest object in view, the billboard for Clayburn Condominiums. "Always seems to come back to you, doesn't it Ross!"

She crossed the lot to a slight rise that overlooked the scene, replaying the action over and over. Whoever it was would have stood about here. Maybe there was a car to help hide behind, no way to find out. Looking across the lot toward the BART station, her eye caught the distinct form of a camera secured high up one of the streetlight poles pointed at her. "Or is there?"

Security cameras are everywhere, and since 9-11 they had multiplied so in some urban areas you're filmed twenty times an hour as you go about minding you own business. She could see three cameras from here. The lot was covered.

O'Mara fished her phone out of her purse.

Six rings. "Kevin, did you check the security cameras in the lot? I'm out here now—there are at least five I can see."

"Yup" He was groggy. "We did indeed. And to the surprise of the BART police, their cameras couldn't see through the rain in their well-lit lot—too much light reflection and visual noise. They did pick up the car and the crime scene as the rain let up but the carjacking was over by then. They caught Franklin in the station and a brief shot of the two kids but that was all. Why the hell are you out there?"

"Did they pick up anyone else?"

"Yeah, there were maybe twenty people who got off the train besides the three of them. The usual mix of professionals and Lafayette types. Nothing suspicious, what are you getting at?"

"The killer, Kevin! Wake up! Franklin was followed by the guy who needed his briefcase. The one who shot the carjacker. We need to see those tapes again. Who's got them?"

"BART police."

"I'll meet you there."

"No you won't. It's one o'clock in the morning. No one who will even think about getting out of bed to find these tapes, not even your lonely Detective Bryan. I'll call in the morning to set up a time to see them."

"Didn't Franklin usually get on at Embarcadero?"

"Yeah, I think so. Why?"

"Did you look at those tapes to see if he was there?"

"No, we only looked at the crime scene tapes, but I see where you're going with this. If he was followed, they picked him up at Embarcadero and waited for the right moment to get the case. Good thinking. You're still not going to get the tapes till tomorrow. Give me a call at nine. Or come on over now to wait. My offer's still on."

"Thanks a lot, but this damn headache is hanging on." The lights from the Clayburn sign lit the way back to her car.

14a

The cell phone punched into her skull like a jackhammer. She rolled over and flipped it open.

"Who the hell is this?"

"Doris Morgan, sorry about the hour."

"Like hell you're. What do you want this time?"

"I need to see you again. I've more information on Cimoni. Can we meet tomorrow, same place and time?"

"No. Did you go to the police like I told you?"

"No, I didn't. I'm scared."

"Tough, unless you do what I told you to do, we can't meet. Not tomorrow or the next day or the next. And don't call me again in the middle of the night. End of conversation."

What's with this woman? Stays up all night worrying about her job and Clayburn? Then calls a total stranger to offer information, most of it circumstantial—well except that bit about Schenk. Why didn't she go to the police? And how the hell did she get my number?

Basil nuzzled up against her arm. "Woke you up too, didn't she fella. She's got no scruples about who she offends." Sharon rolled over and stared at the clock, 3:05, again. She'd been in bed for all of about 30 minutes. At least she's punctual, remembering the last call.

Five hours later O'Mara rolled gallantly into the office, to the shock of her sometime secretary. Messages were piled high, e-mail box full—she hated to deal with those things at home. The top messages were from Anne Franklin, thanking her for the check—as if it was her money—and informing her she had moved permanently to Palm Desert, with new address and phone. O'Mara was sure she didn't need to add them to her address book. The rest were the usual stuff of big companies—

memos, new procedures, revised old procedures, and revised new procedures.

The company newsletter was stuck about halfway down the pile. A face in the top half of the photo of the softball team of the Cincinnati office caught her eye. The tall guy in the middle was a close friend a few years back. Very close, too close just after she had shaken the desert sand out of her hair. He was her boss in the San Francisco office. But when he was moved to Ohio, she stayed in California. His office had won the Cincinnati city corporate softball trophy. She smiled softly, remembering far too much for this time of day. She usually threw the paper out without reading it, but today she turned it over to finish the story. In bold type: **Professional Life to Partner with Clayburn Company of San Francisco to Build Office Condominium Complex.**

I'll be damned, the son of bitch knew about this when we talked and didn't even mention it! Why didn't he mention he was involved with her employer? Might not have made a difference, but it seems important now, almost like an ethical breach. I wonder if the honchos back east in Connecticut know about the connection, or at least the association, between Franklin and Clayburn. I'm sure as hell not going to say anything.

She mentally kicked herself. What connection? This was also circumstantial. None of her research, not even a rumor, put Franklin in Clayburn's pocket. No one knew him. No one had even heard of him.

Her office phone surprised her.

"Good morning, last place I thought I'd find you. Sorry about last night, got a little maudlin. Anyway much better this morning." Kevin's voice and attitude seemed lighter. "Two things. We have an appointment with the BART Police in Oakland at 11:00. They've all the tapes. Since that small riot last year in downtown San Francisco, they've been holding all tapes from all the stations just in case something happens. New policy. A year ago they would have been taped over. Just lucky I guess. We also got a surprisingly quick turnaround on that glass you dropped off yesterday. Things must have been slow in Sacramento. See you in the plaza at the BART Police offices, you know where?"

"Lake Merritt, meet you in the plaza, I'll come in on BART."

At least part of what she heard was good news. Maybe she got a take on Doris Morgan.

14b

Sharon spent the next two hours tidying up the loose ends of three other investigations. One suicide, one accidental workers comp death, and an unfortunate fellow whose tire blew out on 680 at the same time he was trying to pass a truck towing double flat bed trailers. At times her job absolutely sucked. The company expected a complete report for the demographers and statisticians. Every dollar justified and accounted for.

At 10:20 she grabbed her coat and headed to BART, transferred in downtown Oakland, and took the stairs two at a time to the headquarters' plaza. Bryan was sprawled on a south-facing bench, eyes closed to the sun, catching a few mid-winter rays. She kicked his foot.

He squinted. "Hi." She was backlit. He shook his head to clear the vision. "God, you look like a saint. But I knew that all along!"

"Shut up. I head feels more like a sinner after last night. Who are we meeting with?"

"Doug Yamada, good guy, sergeant. Worked with him on a couple of other cases in Lafayette. I called him this morning and he's as anxious as we are to get to the bottom of this. He called about an hour ago saying he'd found the tapes. He subtracted the time from the shooting to the train's arrival to when it left Embarcadero. Everything was there. We're lucky today." Bryan looked toward the west.

"More rain coming! When do we get a break?" He thrust a fist toward heaven. He took in a deep breath and tasted the cool dampness. O'Mara looked into deep gray clouds scudding their way over the two bridges they could see from the headquarters' terrace.

"Just what we need, more rain. And if it isn't rain around here, it's a drought. Nature, God, earth goddess Gaia, somebody just can't seem to get it right. If we get a lot of rain they declare a high fire danger 'cause of the growth. If we don't, it's high fire danger 'cause all that growth is drying out. Hell, we're in California. Fire is like summer—it comes and goes but you can always be sure it will come again."

"Busted, Ms. Sharon O'Mara, professional cynic. Other than the tapes, what's got into you?"

"Awful morning, death and insurance, God I hate it, got to get out. I also found out my employer is a partner in some buildings in the city with Clayburn. No wonder I'm a cynic. I brought some sandwiches.

"Big builders need big money, there you are. What kind?"

"Got three roast beef—cynicism makes me adventurous. Couple of chips and some sodas. Think Yamada will join us?"

"Yep, more than likely. No cop I know can afford to pass up a free meal. Here's another piece of our puzzle. The car that hit Schenk and his friend was an older model Mercedes, black, almost the size of a limousine. A guy across the street saw the whole thing. Unusual car so it caught his eye even before it left the curb. 300 SEL, early 70s, huge front grill, tons of chrome. In these days of cheap plastic boxes, it stood out. You know the car?'

"As a matter of fact, Cimoni drives one. License plate?"

"Nothing positive, too dark and far away. Cimoni, eh? That could make some sense if I didn't think it was the dumbest thing that guy could do. Seems too smart for that type of cheap thuggery."

"Tough to be him anyway—he was beating up that guy by the Opera House about the same time. It's a fast car but he couldn't get from San Francisco to Oakland and back at that time of day without a helicopter. What about my fingerprints?"

"With these new computers and scanners it's amazing! Everything's interconnected! If you've a record, been employed by the government or been in the military, the prints are right there.

Even most of the states are linked in. Jim pulled some nice prints off that glass and sent them on to the state. Got a confirmed response in less than an hour. Here."

Bryan eased a brown envelope toward O'Mara, but kept some pressure on it, so she had to drag it the rest of the way out of his hand. She unfolded the brass clip. The printout was extensive and detailed. First entry: 1990, Tulsa Army Induction Center. They extended through 1999. Then nothing.

"What's this all about, if I may ask? Didn't look too unusual. I've seen a lot like that, no prison or police records, just military and release. You know who that is?"

"Yes!" She was more shocked than Bryan could realize. "Yeah, I know who this is, but they'll be surprised when they find out I know." She pushed the papers back into the envelope and turned to face the police officer that was walking across the plaza to them.

"Hi, Kevin. I assume this is Miss Sharon O'Mara." Doug Yamada wasn't a small man, six-four and easily two hundred and thirty pounds. Trim and sharp, and by O'Mara's trained scan, very fit.

"Yes," Kevin answered. "A professional colleague and friend." He looked chagrined.

"Sandwich, anyone?" she piped, a little too high and too loud.

"If those are roast beef, I'll be ecstatic. Haven't eaten since four this morning. Famished."

"Kevin said you were a good cop, but being able to see through brown bags is a gift." O'Mara felt immediately warm toward Yamada—he was one of the good guys. She pulled the sandwiches from the bag, passed out chips and sodas. Yamada ate like only a cop could eat—large bites and big swallows. The clouds had been building and as they finished, the first drops of rain spotted the paving.

"I have a room set up where we can view the tapes, even make copies of what we need. These damn things are getting better and better. Due to the recent series of muggings and assaults, our customers want the best we can afford. Even the board is having trouble turning down our requests."

Kevin reached for the envelope, but O'Mara was quicker, she shook her head. They followed Yamada into the building. The rain began in earnest, washing the plaza granite. A cold gust of wind pushed them in the door. Winter had returned.

14c

They started with the tapes of the Lafayette parking lot. The cassette had been dated and the time noted from 9:00 PM to 2:12 AM. Yamada commented that the tapes actually ran longer, but the BART investigator pulled the tape and put in a new one.

"Tape? Thought you'd be all electronic by now."

"Coming. By government standards this system is still new. Since 9-11 we're continually under pressure to upgrade, but money also needs to go to the trains—you know, those things the commuters use. So sometimes we have to wait—all digital soon. We're still analog, which is why outdoor resolution is so bad, especially at night."

They fast forwarded to approximately the time of the shooting, no sound, very bright, with a definite pattern of rain slashing upper left to lower right on the screen. The date and time floated in the lower right corner.

"Only one camera in this part of the lot." Yamada apologized.

"But I saw others when I was out there last night."

"Yeah, there are three. One's broken and one was aimed in the wrong direction, so unfortunately just this one. We're also going to install two more."

The image progressively darkened, then almost magically the pictured cleared and an accident appeared on the screen, large car, BMW into the side of a large pickup, Ford; wet pavement and reflections from the parking lot lights framed the scene. Within a few minutes someone walked into the scene and looked inside the cars. They could almost hear the woman's scream.

"She's the one who called it in, or at least ran to the panic button in the lot. We had a squad car there in ninety seconds, he was real close." They watched a squad car pull up, an officer quickly bailed out—obviously talking into his shoulder mike. He checked the interior with a flashlight and spoke again. He pulled the door open and the driver slumped sideways. The officer caught him and pushed him back.

"Bad police work there," city cop to transit cop.

"He didn't know this was a crime scene yet. It's about here he begins to realize something's wrong."

The cop shut the driver's door and walked around the back of the car to check on the passenger. More conversations to his shoulder. He scanned the empty interior of the truck. More headlights and flashing lights start to flare off the hard wet edges in the video.

"The cavalry arrives. This is when Kevin's teams pull up, responding to the panic button and our dispatcher at the same time."

One of the officers points to the right, outside the image, and walks off with two others following him off the screen.

"This is one of the gaps. Franklin was out of the image. We have nothing on tape in that area."

Bryan looked closely at the car. He had seen these tapes once before but now, after his conversation with O'Mara, he was looking for something else, something that wasn't on this tape. They watched until the end, fast forwarding much of the time. Nothing new.

Yamada set up another tape, this one from 9:00 PM to 3:00 AM from the camera in the lobby of the Lafayette station. They watched as the live Franklin walked off the escalator, put on his rubbers, and head directly toward the camera, his hand firmly gripping the briefcase. His face had a distant, eerie gaze in the bright lights of the lobby. Just as he walked out of sight, at the bottom of the screen, the two carjackers bounded down the escalator, one sliding on the handrail—the one who would die.

Their eyes never left Franklin's back. The predators had marked their prey.

They watched the remaining passengers coast down the escalator and out the gate—twelve men, eight women, two carjackers and one Mr. Richard Franklin.

"Doug, Sharon had this flash—and I buy into it—that one of those people may be the one who shot Franklin and the kid and took the briefcase. You recognized any of them?"

"Not right off the bat, Sharon?"

"Go through that tape one more time."

They rolled the tape and could see the faces of all but two people whose faces were covered. One hidden by an umbrella she opened at the foot of the escalator and the other by a large brimmed rain hat. Both were women by their clothing and walk.

"Any tapes from the platform?"

"Nope, that camera was also out that night."

Bryan stomped his foot. "Crazy, I know, but the one with the hat looks familiar—just don't know why."

"You said you had the tape from the Embarcadero Station for this train?" Sharon asked. "The file said that when they checked his BART ticket it was scanned in at the Embarcadero Street station."

"Yes, great idea. We have them from the whole platform I'm told. I haven't seen them, though." He placed another cassette in the machine and started to fast-forward. People scurried back and forth, trains came and went, one bum kept appearing and disappearing.

"Damn, we try to keep that trash out of the station but it's hard, especially in San Francisco where they think this guy has some kind of right to be there. We try to be quiet about getting them out of the station but it's hard, especially on rainy nights." The bum crossed once more, following someone, a woman. Yamada unconsciously slowed the tape. The woman wore a large hat and held her arms tight around her body as she headed toward the line for the next train. She stood stiff, assiduously not looking around, then glanced behind her. The bum was less than a foot away. The wind from the oncoming train briefly lifted the brim of her hat, still too dark to clearly see her face.

The doors slid open. Three men in front of the big hat quickly walked onto the crowded train and the woman followed. The ragman stood at the edge of the platform staring at the woman for a three count beat, then lunged forward, grabbed a dark bundle and pulled his arms out just before the doors closed. He turned and took a step from the edge. The train pulled away. It was obvious the bundle was a bag. He looked into the bag, said something to no one, and threw the bag across the floor. Papers fell out as the bag jammed up against a bench.

They were mesmerized. Bryan asked to fast-forward to just before the next train to Bay Point. Yamada pushed the button and the machine started to speed up.

"Hold it, stop!" yelled O'Mara.

Yamada froze the picture. In mid-stride Franklin was stepping off the escalator.

"Just missed his train," Bryan interpreted. "The poor son of a bitch."

Yamada activated the tape. They watched as Franklin sat down and opened his paper. Another train came into the station blowing papers from the bag toward him. They watched Franklin fold his newspaper and put out his shoe to catch them. He bent over and picked up the torn bag. For the next ten minutes they sat enthralled by Franklin's actions: unwrapping the bag, flattening the pages, scrutinizing of some them. Another train arrived from Oakland. Franklin looked up for a moment, watching people disembark. He turned back to the papers, separated a few, neatly folded them and placed them in his breast pocket.

"I'll be damned! That's how he got the Clayburn papers. The guy had no connection to Clayburn. None!" Sharon said.

Franklin placed the rest of the papers in his briefcase. He looked up and smiled.

"His train is pulling in," Yamada commented.

"Nice smile. I'm starting to like my former client, in spite of his bad taste in wives."

Franklin tucked his newspaper under his arm and headed across the platform to the end of the queue. The crowd from the Oakland train jostled among the waiting passengers. Franklin didn't seem to notice the woman in the big hat and black leather raincoat who walked up behind him.

"That's the woman who was being hassled by the bum," Sharon said. "That's the same woman! She must have turned around at West Oakland, lucky timing to get back here before Franklin and the papers left." Yamada froze the image.

"You're right. Can't miss that hat and the coat. And damn it, she's the one who followed Franklin out of the station in Lafayette." Bryan was gaping at the screen.

"Absolutely," O'Mara confirmed.

Yamada ran the tape in slow motion. Franklin walked toward the platform's edge. Three people stood between him and the hat lady. The train arrived, the doors slid open, Franklin walked on and, to the surprise of the three voyeurs in the dark room, the hat paused before entering the train and looked up into the camera. Light washed across her face.

"Well I'll be damned! If it isn't the delightful and insomniatic Doris Morgan."

Bryan stared, mouth open "No it's not. It's Denise Moran, my overly friendly roommate at the Marriott."

"Roommate?" O'Mara and Yamada both asked—one knowing, the other confused.

"They're both the same person, so where the hell is William Bonney?" Bryan's tone was sarcastic. "Where the fuck is Billy the Kid?"

15a

The midday deluge had abated, but a new early evening front started to spot the Jaguar's windshield, as O'Mara pulled into the illuminated parking lot behind the large billboard displaying Clayburn's new Lafayette apartment complex. The radio announced heavy storms blowing through all night and into tomorrow. O'Mara was getting tired of the mud and a perpetually wet dog; she wondered if spring would ever arrive?

"Damn it," O'Mara spit into her phone.

"Please leave a message, and I'll get right back to you."

"Kevin, call me. I'm in Lafayette at the Clayburn construction site, going to see Cimoni and try to get some answers. Call me."

She stuffed the phone in her rear pocket, while studying the massive structure as she slid out of the car. Lafayette must have been crazy to support such a building. It dwarfed everything along Mt. Diablo Boulevard.

O'Mara had told Bryan the fingerprints came off Morgan's glass. "What the hell," was all he could say, and, "that son of a bitch better stay out of my way." After he compared what he now knew about Morgan/Moran with the fingerprint report he called Clayburn to see if Morgan was there. She hadn't shown up that morning, not a word since yesterday. It was unusual for her not to report in. After a brief phone call to the district attorney, Bryan and Yamada decided to get a warrant for her arrest.

O'Mara had stopped in at her office, for the second time in one day—just one phone message. A woman's voice, muffled, but maybe Morgan's, asked her to meet Cimoni at the construction trailer in Lafayette at 7:30. He wanted "to set the record straight." What record, she wasn't sure. She knew Cimoni had setup and played Schenk. She was also sure much of Pell's current net worth was due to the generosity of Clayburn and Cimoni, but so were a lot of other politicians, so leave the poor guy alone—his wife's dying. All threads to Franklin had now dissolved. Like a puzzle, the more you looked at the pieces the more easily and quickly they fit together. Turning the few remaining pieces might finish the picture.

O'Mara sloshed through the muddy lot toward the bright lights of the trailer at the front of the dimly illuminated construction. She climbed the temporary wood stair and knocked on the metal door, kicking the mud off her boots.

"Yeah, yeah, come in," a gruff voice called through the steel.

Cimoni was standing behind a large desk covered with plans, his back to the wall, cell phone to one ear. He looked surprised to see her, but didn't miss a beat. "Good evening Ms. O'Mara, be with you in a minute."

Rainwater ran off her slicker and dripped on the dusty floor.

"Yes, I heard you Fred. I know you wanted to save me some money with that fitting, but it's not in the plans and it doesn't meet the specs. Make it the same as the documents and we won't have a problem . . . I don't care what you thought, your contract says what is correct and that's what you'll provide. They'll be here in two days or you risk your contract . . . right . . . right . . . Yeah, yeah, talk to you later." Cimoni hung up.

"You handle all your subs that way?"

"Only those that try to jerk me around. Kind of like you, only different. What the hell you doing here?" Cimoni's battered face, still black-and-blue, toughened up his character a bit.

"Well, Mr. Opera Hero, I'm here because you asked me to meet you. Or at least your assistant did. So what's so important other than what I already know? You and Schenk—was quite an evening after the meeting."

"You don't know anything and I didn't ask you here. Nor did I ask anyone else to ask you here. That ass Schenk got what he deserved, but you, you've been poking your nose around here for weeks, stirring up all sorts of trouble, and you still don't know anything." He looked directly at her; his hands grasped the edge of the desk. His knuckles, white.

"Well you're probably right. All those things I learned about Schenk and his hooker would probably fall on deaf ears, especially police ears. All those things suggest extortion, bribery, campaign funds, fraud, and, for good measure, attempted murder might be ignored by the police. Hell, I'll bet not one of those would probably stick to you. But for fun, let's find out. Which one do you like? Let me throw it and see if it sticks."

"Yeah, sure. Bribed who? What hooker? Extorted who? Killed who?"

"Let's just say that development is a tough game, and any leverage that can be brought to bear is helpful. Right so far?" She moved deeper into the room, leaving a wet trail across the floor.

"Leverage is part of it, Ms. O'Mara. Information is also part of it. And money is the glue that binds it all together. Take you for instance—I know you're an insurance investigator. I also know you were a cop in the Army and spent some time in Iraq, sometimes dealing with the dark secrets everyone carries."

She looked surprised.

"I get information too—old and new. From my contacts I know you're very good at what you do, but I'm surprised you've bit into this as hard as you have. It doesn't concern you. Franklin was an unfortunate bloke in the wrong place at the wrong time, a poor fool whose curiosity got the best of him. Schenk was as righteous as he wanted everyone to believe, but his dick led him around." Cimoni walked around the desk and leaned against its front edge.

"It's important to know all I can, especially if that rich ass I work for is offering you a job. You're a threat. As such I've to deal with you as an enemy. Information is the key to my business."

She laughed at his seriousness. To him people were no more than pawns in his weird little game of competition and success.

"A threat? How can I be a threat to you or to Clayburn? What I know anyone can find out. When these accidents are linked together, someone will discover there's more going on. More like murder—murder by intent and sick desire. Come on Cimoni, your well-manicured hands are all over this."

"Murder, what the hell are you talking about?" He stood upright. The low trailer ceiling added drama to the gesture.

"There are four dead citizens, some connected to Clayburn and you. The only innocent person was Franklin. Fine. Everyone else had something to gain. The dead kid wanted Franklin's car. Schenk wanted power and a free piece of ass. Leanne Wu, the hooker, wanted your money. Franklin was the only one who had nothing to gain. And in the end that's exactly what he got—nothing."

"Who is this Leanne Wu?" He sounded a bit too innocent.

"Oh, come now, Cimoni, you could have at least remembered her name. You were the one who so graciously introduced her to Schenk. It was your need to know about your enemies that got you the information about his penchant for Orientals. Once you had him hooked," she smiled at her joke, "you twisted him into such a knot, he compromised GRIPE's position on your project. Oh, he sounded like he'd done some homework, but it was your hooker who extorted that speech from him. In fact, I'll bet that parking lot brawl was staged just so his followers would see how deep his convictions were. Yes. His convictions were all in his pants, and you used that girl to get to those convictions."

"Great story. You should write fiction. You're very good at it." He turned his back on her, walked back behind the table. "Where did you gather all these supposed facts?"

"As you said information is king. There are some people who don't like you or your style. People you've screwed at one time. People who'd willingly point a finger at you if asked. The information they gave me says you're not a very nice guy, Allen. They say you could even murder people." Her bluff cracked his shell.

"Who the says that?" He paused for a moment, then smiled. "Morgan! That bitch! She called you, she told you these stories. Are you here to extort money from me, like Pell? He was willing to sell himself, to sell his trust for money. Whether he needed it or not is irrelevant. He put his name and honor up for sale—and I bought it. Cheap. Damn cheap! I don't see it the same way you do. Is that what you want? Silence for money? I've already spent a fortune on silence—you're not the first with their hand out. Sweetie, the line forms at the rear."

"You saying someone else is extorting you?" She couldn't cover her surprised.

"Yeah, someone who sends me bits and pieces of letters, checks, and photos of my political and social dealings. Embarrassing dealings—half a check, a photo of me and someone cut off. My security people watch everything—even me. Nothing. They've found nothing. It's like someone knew what I was doing and where I was all the time. Where the hell they got those papers, I haven't a clue. But I've shelled out thousands to keep him quiet. For a while I thought it was you—that's how paranoid I've become. Now I know it's Morgan. No one else has access to all that information, information that could send a few people to prison if it got out. So O'Mara, how much do you want? Ten thousand, twenty? I need this project. Your costs would be minor in the end. I'll deal with Morgan on my own."

"I don't want your money, I only want the truth. Look, Cimoni, someone tried to kill me too. Do you know how that feels? Anyone ever try to kill you, Cimoni?

"How noble. The truth. How many have used that excuse to get what they wanted? It's revenge you want. Give me truth so I can face reality. Hah! What you really want is an excuse to justify your actions. Truth? You want truth? I'll give you truth." His fury reverberated off the metal walls. "I didn't run over Schenk or his hooker, but for what I got from Schenk, she was cheap. I still don't know who the hell Richard Franklin is. I suggest the truth starts with that bitch of an assistant Morgan. There, that's the truth! So what does the truth gain you? You're no further ahead than before you came through that door."

"That's where you're wrong, Cimoni. I'm much further ahead than when I came through that door." O'Mara's phone began to buzz.

"You better answer that, before it sets your butt on fire."

She checked the display. "Kevin, I'm at the Clayburn construction site. Yeah, talking to Cimoni, . . . yes . . . yes . . . soon. Good." She pushed the phone back in her pocket.

"Boyfriend?" His voice had a wicked edge.

"This afternoon I had a good idea who killed those people, now I'm sure. You're a son of a bitch and you know it, but I doubt you have the balls to kill anyone. It's not your style, but it is someone else's. And, by the way, I'll bet you didn't know Doris Morgan's original name was Dennis Moran? Tulsa boy, ex-army, probable sex change, bad temper, nice ass, and worked on projects with a certain Allen Cimoni in the orient."

"Moran! No fucking way."

"Way."

15b

The rain increased its tattoo on the metal roof to a dull roar. O'Mara saw the carnage before she heard the muffled crack of the rifle over all the din. The window to her left blew out, showering glass and rain into the room. Cimoni's eyes opened wide in surprise before his head spun to the left throwing black hair and pink brain matter on the wall. What was left of Cimoni bounced off the wall and splayed, arms wide, across the blueprints on the desk. Blood and tissue continued to spurt over the plans as his heart refused to die.

O'Mara dove toward the door, hitting the light switch on her way to the muddy floor—a millisecond before the window next to her exploded. On a three count another bullet pierced the wall and exited to her right, leaving a laser-like shaft of light casting a white spot on the opposite wall. That spot and the light from the shattered windows were all that illuminated the room.

A fish in a barrel—a goddamn fish in a fucking barrel. Another crack and the coffee pot exploded spewing glass and hot coffee on her back. Another shaft of light illuminated the room. She crawled toward the door, took a deep breath, sprung to her feet, pulled the door open and leaped into the darkness. The rifle cracked again. The bullet found her. The searing pain in her left shoulder left no doubt who had reached the door first.

She rolled through the mud and yanked the Beretta from the holster under her slicker. Her shoulder burned with a fire she hadn't felt in years. Bolting to her feet she fled to the relative safety of the leeward side of the trailer. It's tougher to hit something you can't see. O'Mara set the pistol on the edge of the dark wood steps, her hand searched for the pain in her shoulder. The intense heat of the wound was wearing off. Her arm and shoulder still moved—no major damage, maybe a nick. She knew she would get shocky in a few minutes, adrenaline pumped through her holding it at bay. She had to act before her body became her primary enemy.

She picked up the pistol, flicked the safety, and ran to the far end of the trailer. Hidden in shadows, she looked across the construction site. The rain provided some cover. No movement. The marksman had to be higher than the trailer, maybe in the building. But how high and where? And he was dry. She was soaked, muddy, and probably bloody. The Jag sat in the driveway, fully lit. No point in trying to get out that way.

The only route was between the piles of wood forms to the opening in the basement. A single bulb there outlined the door. One . . . two . . . a third deep breath and she zigzagged through slippery mud. At the dry doorway she stopped. The rifle cracked and she looked toward the parking lot. Her car, outlined in the reflected glow from the structure, stood alone, undefended, exposed. First the new rear window crazed and collapsed. Then, in rapid succession, under the unrelenting fusillade of a fully automatic weapon, the Jaguar collapsed on its rims as the wheels exploded, the bonnet flew up and the remaining windows shattered into a thousand shards— an AK-47. Even after all those years, she knew the sound deep in her soul. Her heart flooded with fury. For a moment the wounded car crouched in the rain like the animal it was named for. Then it erupted into a fireball.

Even the rain didn't lessen the intensity. O'Mara staggered back from the shock wave of heat.

"What the hell do you have against my car, Morgan? That's twice you've shot it. This time you killed it." The drumming of the rain and the roar of the fire was all the response she received.

"I know it's you, Morgan. At least let me know I'm right," she hollered up into the empty building hoping for an answer, hoping for a target, hoping for anything.

O'Mara retreated into the relative dryness of the dim garage. Light pierced the space from safety lamps mounted in the floor above. She could make out what was what by their shadows. There were no solid forms, only ghosts.

She clung to the wall. The mud helped blacken out the light color of her clothing. She scraped mud from her pants and rubbed it on her face. She tasted blood mixed with construction dust. At least her hair was pulled back, away from her face. The pain forced her to think slowly through all her actions.

A slight scrape on wood overhead forced O'Mara to move along the wall toward the stairway washed in light from above. Nothing going up or down would make it three steps. Morgan knew the building, she didn't. There were only three things she could do—go up the stairs and come down a twisted pile of meat. Stay where she was until Morgan found her. Or go outside and work around and up to the entry, a flanking move. You learn that early in military training.

O'Mara stayed in the shadows, slid along the wall toward the other garage exit. The rain was a sheet hung across the opening. Above, the headlights on the adjacent Highway 24 flashed through the loud gauze. Standing in the blackness next to the doorway, she clicked the pistol's safety off and on and felt for the backup clip in her pocket next to her phone. At least she could pull it out with her left hand. It would be impossible to reload one handed.

The walls flanking the driveway and the ramp sloped up into the obscuring rain. Couldn't run to the end of the ramp, too exposed. She looked at the five-foot wall next to the building—her shoulder would make her scream with agony, but it was the only way out of here. O'Mara put the pistol in its holster and moved a sawhorse against the wet wall. The rain etched her shoulder like daggers. She could feel the mud washing away, could feel herself becoming visible. She hoisted herself up and over the wall onto a pile of construction debris, rested in the shadow of the building, panting, hidden, still sixty feet from the front entry—waiting for the agony to ease.

She crawled along the base of the wall. Her shoulder was stiffening and the adrenaline hit was wearing off. From the entry, all she could make out was iron scaffolding—scant protection against an automatic weapon. Slipping into the building, she hid under the scaffolding, listening. No sound, only rain. From the angle of the first volley of shots, Morgan must be on the second floor. She guessed Morgan was still up there, but where exactly? No clue. Likely Morgan would catch her if she started to climb. Always hold higher ground. They'd both learned that, in the same school. O'Mara needed to end it here. To end it here, there was only one way—she needed the higher ground.

She reached for her pistol and inched herself along the wall, leaving a trail like a slug that marked her passage through the dust.

Probing with her toe, she found the first tread and began the silent step-by-step climb.

She knew this is how a condemned man feels climbing the scaffold. She hoped there were more than thirteen steps. Kneeling on the second floor landing, she tried to contain her breath and stretch out the fire in her shoulder. The landing was clear. The AK-47 barked again and echoed against the harsh surfaces. A bullet ripped through the wall next to her head. Morgan had also moved.

Four rapid shots ripped through the hallway, walls, and floor of the landing. Chalk from the drywall covered everything, turning the kneeling figure into a ghostly fish—still in a barrel. If she'd been standing, she would be dead. Knowing where Morgan had set up shop was not a lot of help. Two more probing bullets exploded through the wall, hoping to find her exact location. And that was the good news?

O'Mara dove through the first doorway, rolled into the room. She clenched her teeth to ride out the pain. Plaster stuck to her wet clothes—if she didn't move quickly, she'd become a real ghost.

"Come on O'Mara." The voice was down the hallway. "Give it up. You're mine, you're already dead. Accept it."

"Stealing my lines, Morgan—or is it Moran tonight? I'm the one who says give it up. You're the one who has no future." She rolled tightly into a corner. "You've killed five people—for what? Money, revenge, sex—whatever sex you're today? Or is it all the usual bullshit and excuses? What in the hell did they do to you?"

A roar of explosions and bullets tore through the room, inches above her head—Morgan had moved down to her level.

"What the hell," O'Mara yelled, and fired three shots out the door and down the hall.

"Wondering when you would get around to that." Morgan taunted. "Missed me. All that training, it seems, wasted."

Wiping water and plaster sludge from her eyes, O'Mara saw another shape, opposite of the muzzle flashes. Two people—who? What? Another flash, another explosion. "I see you, bitch."

O'Mara gripped the Beretta and dove across the hall, firing as she hit the floor. Morgan's AK-47 traced O'Mara's rolling form. A bullet in her thigh sent lightning up her leg. Pain locked her lungs. No sound forced itself through the dust that filled her mouth. She saw Morgan stagger, push away from the drywall. Even in the dim haze, O'Mara could see blood spraying from Morgan's flayed side. Morgan dropped the empty assault rifle, steadied herself, and pulled a chrome pistol from her waist. With a shaking two-handed grip she aimed at the crumpled ghost. O'Mara looked past Morgan to the black shape in the doorway, wide-stance, a glint flashing from his praying hands. The explosion blinded and dazed her—but not enough to miss seeing Doris Morgan slam against the wall, scream an unholy howl and slide to the floor like a bag of rags. Bryan eased into the room still gripping his service pistol, braced for another shot if needed. His gaze was locked on Morgan. He moved toward her and kicked her pistol across the chalky floor. She stared at him, blinking dust from her eyes. Her mascara didn't run; her thick makeup was too perfect.

O'Mara braced herself, inching her way toward Bryan, found purchase and pulled herself up.

Morgan lay against a bucket of trash, one arm dangling loosely over its edge.

"Why all this, Morgan? What for?" O'Mara's voice was breaking up. Bryan put his arm under hers, his phone to his ear. "I need EMT's here, now! Same location, now! Two down, now, goddamnit," Bryan hollered, even as sirens started up in the distance.

Morgan coughed, dark matter trailed from the corner of her mouth, "They were in the way, between me and Cimoni. I wanted him to suffer, to loose it all, to wish he was dead. It was working, too, until that creep in the BART station and that nosey accountant found them." Morgan tried to stand, only to collapse back into the dust.

"Come on, girly-boy," O'Mara goaded. "There was no way you could have shook him up that much—he was too arrogant." Plaster and water dripped in long viscous strings down her face forming eerie white circles of slurry that glowed in the construction lights. O'Mara kept jerking her leg to escape the burning pain. Bryan slowly lowered her to the floor, till she was eye to eye with Morgan.

"Oh I could." Morgan's coughing choked her words. "I knew stuff about him that would have made your soggy red hair stand up on end. He should live in a rat hole hotel in the Tenderloin, not on Russian Hill. He was a swindler, set up fake companies that took in investors, and then ran out. That's who he was when I met him. He knew me as Dennis Moran then." She looked at Bryan with a twisted smile. "By the way, never told you, nice ass Bryan boy. Really nice." Her breathing was choppy, she gulped of air.

"Good story," O'Mara began to drift. "Fits nicely, too nicely. You were doing us all a favor by killing him. But why?"

The rain continued to beat heavily on the roof, the sirens and blue and white flashes bounced off the walls. Morgan's voice got louder.

"A deal. He set up a deal in Manila. I set up connections for him, put in all my money. He split, I was broke. Ever tasted debt, honey? I got locked up. Not fun in Asia. Swore one day I'd cut the balls off that pig. Why couldn't you have left all this alone, O'Mara? I actually took a liking to you—but I warned you at the site, tried to scare you off. Why the hell are you dogging this?"

"What did you have against my car?"

"That piece of English crap. I had a Jaguar in Hong Kong, same color. It never ran, sucked all my cash, left an oil trail everywhere. Every time I shot your car, Ms. O'Mara, it was a fantasy come true, a real fucking fan-ta-cee."

Morgan's head rolled to one side, eyes still open, her lifeless arms hung at her side, one leg propped against the white bucket. O'Mara reached out, closed Morgan's eyes, and passed out.

15c

O'Mara sluggishly reached for the screaming rod and reel. The fish jumped, flew through the haze of her vision. She arched back on the rod and was hard on to the fish. It pulled, she braced, tasted salty sweat on her upper lip. The intense heat made her thirst unquenchable. She hauled back and reeled, yet the line flew from the reel in an endless cry. She couldn't stop the fish, couldn't turn it, couldn't even slow it down. She turned to the deck hand—it was Cimoni with half his head gone. Her arms ached, the sea turned blood red, splashed crimson gore on her bare arms and legs. The fish still danced across the fiery sea. The white-hot sun drained her strength, sucked away her life. For three days she fought against that fish that wanted to pull her into the bloody sea. Slowly the sun darkened and cooled, and in the haze of the boundless red sky, a dark face materialized.

"Hi. How are you feeling?" the face asked. Sharon tried to get her brain to focus on what her eyes were seeing, try and bridge the chasm. "Glad to see you're back with us. We were all worried, especially Basil. He didn't want to go with me to my dump. You just rest, I'll be back." The face disappeared and the sun filled her horizon. Kevin turned it out as he left the room.

O'Mara once felt better than she did right now, but it was hard to remember when. There was a time when breathing didn't hurt and she could walk to the bathroom, not want to crawl. It hurt just to move. The doctor said the slug had done a fair amount of damage to her upper leg, but nothing major was severed or broken. She'd need months of rehab to strengthen the tortured muscles. She had lost a lot of blood through the nick in her shoulder. She had never really cared about her hands and nails, but now they looked like she'd dug, bare handed, her own grave. With all this time on her hands (she laughed at her own joke) she would finally have time for a manicure.

Kevin came daily with flowers and candy. O'Mara—scraped, wounded, and famished—hoped for carbonara and a cigarette. She said thanks, but he insisted she stay in bed during their date. Kevin was happy—he'd never had a date began and end in bed—he usually never even saw the bedroom.

"Morgan killed them all," he reported. "Now we know it's her, that's no surprise. She accumulated copies of all of Cimoni's dealings to blackmail him—her place was full of them. Clayburn's accountants think it may have been almost one hundred thousand over three years—small payments here and there, nothing that seemed to alert them, no flags, Cimoni covered the expenses. Poor dope didn't seem to have a clue who was doing it. Clayburn still denies knowing anything about anything—and he looks pretty clean, as far as it goes. The papers Franklin picked up off the floor did end up in her place. Somehow one of his Starbucks Visa receipts got stuck in with the copies—it was in her apartment."

"Who killed Franklin?" interrupted O'Mara.

"Not sure who killed who in the BART lot, but it could have easily been Morgan who killed them both. Yeah, it could have happened that way, but the bullets are too damaged to tell. Her AK-47 matches the caliber of the holes in your Jag. By the way—sorry about that. I know she was your best buddy after Basil and me. By the time the fire department arrived, all that was left burning were the tires. What's left is in the impound lot. She's gone."

"Thanks for your concern." She groaned, broken hearted. "Schenk?"

"She probably ran over him and Wu with Cimoni's Mercedes. His car matches the one that hit them, almost a positive. The techs pulled some evidence from the bumper, a piece of a shirt with a whale on it—go figure. No blood or DNA though. It's like a tank; a new car would have folded on impact. She took his car out of the company garage—they found it leaving on closed circuit tape—couldn't identify the driver, though—too dark. She tried to pin the hit-and-run on Cimoni. He had FasTrak and we timed his car crossing the bridge back into San Francisco twenty minutes after they were hit. Cimoni was going one-on-one with the bum that jumped him. Didn't miss it."

"We also think she was the one who setup Schenk for Cimoni," Kevin continued. "Cimoni thought he was running Wu, when it was really Morgan. Not getting the rap to stick to him must have really pissed Morgan off. She really wanted him to suffer in prison, like she had. Full-on humiliation! Herman Pell still has a lot of questions to answer. He's probably off to jail sometime in the future. It's a bitch too—they told me his wife died two days ago."

"Can't believe she actually said she liked me!" Sharon said. "Strange dude. Crisply calm on the outside—actually too crisp. And all that seething rage beneath the skin, whatever flavor she was. Kev?"

"Yeah?"

"Thanks for showing up when you did."

"I'm glad you called, but next time give me more notice. I

hate playing Sir Galahad when there's so much blood already flowing."

"Sorry, can't say I planned it that way."

"Her last few years as Dennis Moran though were very interesting. The Army has him in a special operations branch, one that was scuttling around the Middle East and Far East. Clandestine and dark ops stuff, that's all we could find out. Later he was involved in some real estate deals in the Philippines, with some big money, money they're not sure where he got it. After those deals went south, he disappeared. Actually there was a report he may have fallen off a ferry there. Disappeared, as they say. The autopsy explains why. There was little that remained of the original Dennis Moran. Coroner says it was a good job, could have fooled anyone. And I was one lucky son of a bitch as well. During the check of her place I found another envelope with a collection of even more flattering pictures of me: silk ties, the hotel room, bizarre toys, and a woman. No face, just a woman's body in all sorts of interesting poses. Good lord, he even kissed me. I assume he was saving them as insurance. Hell I don't know—really, really, stupid on my part. The captain let me keep them before they got all over the place; I burned 'em."

"Yuck!" Sharon said forcing a smile. "By the way, I made copies of the ones she left at my place."

"There was no sign of him until the fingerprints you took showed up in Washington," Bryan said, ignoring her remark. "Why she wasn't more careful about her prints and that glass we'll never know. She wiped the briefcase but left her prints for you – just forgot I guess. No other inquires. Clayburn admits being a little lax in his research when she was hired. He says she just had a good grasp of reality, something he really liked about her. Raves about her as an employee, loyal and thorough. And she knew her way around the Far East.

"Ran back here to San Francisco to get away from it all, maybe," O'Mara added. "Then Cimoni shows up, cuts in line, and she starts to seethe. Her whole scam was methodical and she didn't like me sticking my nose into her little party. One very confused and pissed off man or woman."

"Hey, I picked up your mail. Not much, a few cards and an envelope from your company." She pulled out a check and read the letter.

"Those sons of bitches have fired me! Stuff about procedures, impact on current cases within the company, unacceptable professionalism, their reputation compromised. Basically I'm an embarrassment to them. It seems, I guess, they can't have a real investigator on their staff—one who finds answers, one who carries a gun. Well, screw-em." O'Mara flipped the letter to the floor, making sure it didn't include her last check.

"When I'm well enough, I'm off to the East Cape of Cabo. Sun, tequila and marlin, that's what I want: find my tan, brush up on my Spanish, and troll deep blue saltwater. A few weeks would just be great."

Exhausted, she took Bryan's hand. He raised it further and kissed the tips of her fingers. Smiling, her eyes slowly closed. The medical lamp still blazed through her eyelids as if the sun stood motionless in the high sky. She drifted back to sleep.

The End

About the Author:

Gregory C. Randall, Midwesterner by birth, Californian by choice, has lived in the same town as Sharon O'Mara for over twenty years. Old enough to be her father, he is enjoying the chance to share her life with our readers and fans. Greg is continuing to work on the next adventures for Sharon and she is excited to be part of his family. Greg is also an author of other works in non-fiction and fiction.

The Flyer

I have tried to pare these stories in a manageable length that you can read in less than eight hours, at 65,000 words the idea is that you can read about half the book on a four hour flight and the rest on the way home. I call them Flyers. If you aren't flying, settle back, pour a good drink and enjoy.

Connect with Greg online:
www.gregorycrandall.com
Follow the development of the next
Sharon O'Mara Chronicle at
www.writing4death.blogspot.com

Other books by Mr. Randall
Fiction
Elk River

The Sharon O'Mara Chronicles
Land Swap For Death
Containers For Death
Toulouse For Death
12th Man For Death

Non-fiction
America's Original GI Town, Park Forest, Illinois

Additional copies can be purchased through these sites as well as through the usual on-line bookstores.